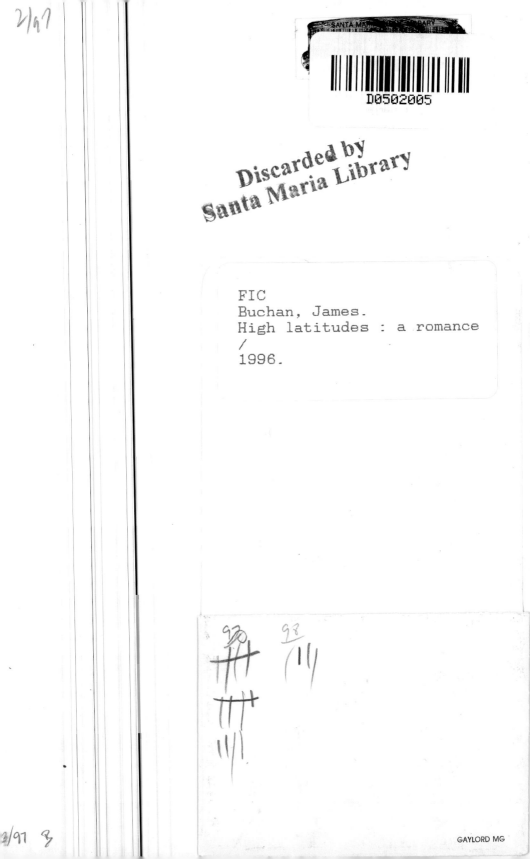

2/97

GAYLORD MG

3/97 3

HIGH LATITUDES

FARRAR
STRAUS
GIROUX

HIGH LATITUDES

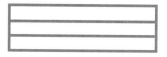

A Romance

JAMES BUCHAN

Farrar Straus Giroux

NEW YORK

To Mr. and Mrs. Daniel Weinstein of Jamestown, New York

Library of Congress Cataloging-in-Publication Data

Buchan, James.
High latitudes : a romance / James Buchan. — 1st American ed.
p.   cm.
ISBN 0-374-16999-3 (alk. paper)
1. Women in business—Great Britain—Fiction.   2. Divorced
women—Great Britain—Fiction.   I. Title.
PR6052.U215H5   1996
823'.914—dc20   96—17250
                                                  CIP

HIGH LATITUDES

*One night I dreamed that Burlington Street
was full of ice blocks and that I was
navigating a ship along it . . .*

Worsley

I

Imagine a shopping street in the West End of London: not Burlington Street, necessarily, but parallel to or running across it. Make it lunchtime, to give you crowds, hurry, hunger and a holiday so short it exasperates. Amid the tide of men and women, set down some reefs and wrecks: people who don't work in offices or shops, who have no job or money to buy anything, or have a job but it is handing out leaflets for nightclubs or free hair-cuts, or gulling tourists; or who stand four-square on the pavement before windows full of electrical goods, shouting, Everything must go! We lost our lease!; as if there ever had been a lease to the store, which was opened that previous midnight, not even swept but stacked to the ceiling with black boxes from South Korea and dolls from Taiwan, and would trade just so long as the police could be persuaded; as if, in short, the world had been created this moment, but with an inventory of fabricated memory.

Into these flows and eddies of people, introduce a young woman, walking, eyes to the pavement, lost in thought or not even thinking. Put her there because the fate of a beautiful woman is still of greater interest to the readers of romances than the fate of squatting electrical retailers and because I want you to see Jane Haddon, as she is now, in the autumn of 1987, without her self-consciousness. Jane's hair is black, and cut short, no doubt to make her look boyish; and she wears a matching jacket and skirt, also black, and made for her by her ex-husband's tailor in the Corso d'Italia in Turin; which suit, though it cost her the equivalent of a thousand pounds and will cost twelve hundred pounds to replace, she will go on having made until she or the tailor are dust; for it is a decision Jane has taken.

Jane moves in the crowds, as a fox in standing wheat or a royal person at a supermarket opening. To her they are noiseless, motive and invisible, like wind to a sail-boat. She moves in the eye of this narrative and also in the eye of Stephen Cohen, who is leaning against the plate glass of Tempo Computers across the street, precisely so he can see her thus: where she can't answer back or disturb, by word or gesture, his deep-laid plans; where Jane is his flag, colonising an alien territory. She turns into a restaurant and Stephen runs across the traffic. A despatch rider leans, swears, pulls away. And as the door of the restaurant closes on the tumult, as she turns startled among the waitresses, and smiles, as her public nature comes down like a shutter, Stephen says:

"Help me, Jane."

The brush of her cheek is too sudden for him to record.

"I'll try," she says.

If Jane has a fault in Stephen's eye, it is that she has no moral spontaneity: she is virtuous and amiable, but only because she has decided to be so; and might, just as decisively, have been a thief or whore. Her suit, though practical to the point of uniform, now seems to Stephen itself an affectation: a criticism of fashion, even of femininity. Seated across the table, she is businesslike and widow-black; though her right hand flicks open the bound list of wines, her eye floats over it and back to Stephen, as if to say, Funny, all these wines, and at lunch!

At this moment, Stephen is interested in what she decides to do. If Jane says:

"We're sharing this, I take it, Stephen," it means she wants to drink some wine – say, the Château Angélus of 1982, which is expensive or cheap depending on your circumstances but by any standard of life or literature a good wine – her work is going well and the lunch sheds some of its commercial character. Troublesome things – friendship, a shared history, sex – come sliding in.

She says: "I think it's my turn, Stephen, isn't it?"

"No, absolutely not. I insist. And anyway, I feel like something fabulous. You choose."

"I have a buyers' meeting at Reuben & Style. I'll shine," she says, and will; and, as if to restore a businesslike sobriety, "What can I do for you, Stephen?"

"You can write to Johnny."

"I believe I said, Stephen, that it was none of my business."

"They're all fucking crooks, Jane!"

"And so?"

In the busy restaurant, Jane was smoking a cigarette: a disreputable habit in a woman of her age. She said through her smoke, "I refuse to talk further either about Lloyd's or my ex-husband and, if you want to, you'll have to do so to somebody else." She put on an official sort of smile. "You mentioned a property on the phone."

"Near Padua. Bed and bath . . ."

"Not a good start. And the price, if I may ask?"

"Twenty-four times its 1986 earnings, but management expects growth of fifteen per cent this year and next, and, Jane! Italy!"

Translated out of business jargon, that meant: Stephen was offering Jane, on behalf of its owners, a factory on the Adriatic coast manufacturing sheets and towels and for a price equivalent to a multiple of twenty-four times its annual profits (which, it being Italy, the cradle of scientific book-keeping, Stephen suggested were artificially reduced to avoid income taxes. Now no rational person would take on an enterprise that would only earn its living in its twenty-fifth year, except perhaps a woman of child-bearing age.)

"I'm not buying anything, even from you, on a price/earnings multiple of twenty-four."

"Hell, Jane, Nippon Telegraph was sold on two hundred and . . ."

"It is simply not possible for me to operate a business that earns – what's the reciprocal of twenty-four expressed as a percentage . . ."

"Four point two per cent . . ."

". . . that earns four per cent, when my capital costs me fourteen per cent." She looked down at her wine and said, "I'd be a seller at these prices. Even of Motherwell. You should be aware of that." She looked up, winningly, and said, "How's Lizzie?"

Lizzie was Stephen's girlfriend, and the question a flirtation: a trifle before parting, but still a little commercial in quality, like the fortune cookies that had come with the bill.

"She's fine, Jane. Thank you for asking."

On the pavement, Stephen missed again the texture of her cheek. She walked away into the crowds – not working-people now, but the permanent day-time swell of jobless and homeless and moneyless, the miserable and the rich, the junkies and boozers and tourists and time-killers – and Stephen thought: At some point, fear will get the better of you, fear of getting old and losing your looks and being alone and dying. Then you'll be pleased that I'm still here, Janet McKay.

Then he captured a taxi and, as it bounced down High Holborn and across the ditch of Farringdon Street into the City, he pondered what Jane had said about the price of the Zampieri mill and other industrial properties; and, back at his office at S.L. Brimberg, he telephoned the stockbrokers on the floor below and the chairman's secretary on the floor above, and sold every industrial security he owned and a great many that he did not own, wrote two letters in his own hand, telephoned New York and Chicago, and then, even though it was not yet five o'clock, left with a small bag for the country. Riding the tube to King's Cross, he felt not relief at a week's work done or the pleasure of social anticipation, but shame: as if he had ripped Jane's shirt from her neck and breast. Stephen Cohen thought himself an all-right guy and a better investment banker, but he'd never met anybody like Jane.

Jane was two minutes late for the buyers' conference at Reuben & Style. The meeting room, as she strode in, was precisely as she'd imagined it in those two minutes: Alan Nixon up at a blackboard, racks of slips and underwear on castors, young men and women in R & S suits and coats and skirts positioned against the walls. Alan was writing the word VAT? on the blackboard in purple chalk.

"I thought you were hanging on to that, Alan."

Jane hated to be late. She added:

"It's not as if the public will pay another eighteen per cent. And I, Alan, will go bust."

The British government, which had a parliamentary majority of four and a horror of raising income taxes, had just imposed a sales tax known as Value Added Tax on newspapers, books, children's dentistry and optical medicine, and all underwear.

Alan Nixon turned round. Inasmuch as he entertained any feeling towards Jane as a person, as distinct from her character as managing director of a large and uppity supplier, Alan detested Jane. This was not because she was a woman. Reuben & Style had always favoured women in the business, or at least since the First World War, when men were in short supply and Simon Reuben and Jack Style broke with the tradition of low pay for females in the distributive trades. "There seems to your directors to be no commercial reason," Simon told the Annual General Meeting in 1917, "why modest and hard-working girls should not enjoy all the benefits of our best men." Why, three of the store managers were now women – Edinburgh, Princes Street; Chester; and Swansea – there was a woman director on the board and this room, just above the traffic on Marylebone Road, was more than half-filled with women in their staff-discounted suits, looking at Jane with an expanded reflection of their chairman's disapproval, though tinged with an intense and, because for a mere supplier, guilty admiration.

Nor was it because Jane had been a countess; for though Simon had politely refused a marquisate from Lloyd George's agent – at one hundred thousand pounds in 1919 money, it was way above market – he'd been followed, in the ripeness of time, by Lords Style, Secker, Ryman and MacArtnay – their names exemplifying the slow gentilisation of the business – and would be, no doubt, when the time came and Australia was sorted out and Germany came right, by Lord Nixon of Crawley. Nor was it even because Jane, as managing director of a company with seventy thousand employees and four thousand million pounds in capital employed, was a little too powerful for the purposes of Reuben & Style; if she'd been much weaker, as Alan himself recognised, she would have been no use.

It was not because she wasn't plain, because the entire female working class of Britain and Ulster was rattling at the doors of Reuben & Style and, ever since Simon's day, it had been not exactly the policy of floor managers, but rather their predilection to hire, all other things being equal and congruent with the practices of the finest business in the British Isles, the prettiest. It was not because Jane was intelligent, because so was Alan, and every young woman and man in the room; and if their intelligence was a little narrow, focused as it was on the stock-checking lists that peeped, even now, out of Alan's pre-display suit coat pocket – Jane recognised the rings in red ink where he had noted a discrepancy between a product's share of floor space and its contribution to gross turnover – well, Jane knew her stock-checking lists.

Alan disliked Jane because she had been to university, and Alan had not, having joined Glasgow, Queen Street at fourteen; nor had any of his pantheon of retailers, or any other man or woman in the room I'm describing five floors above the Marylebone Road, except Jane. I think there must have been times when Alan, kissing his children goodnight or sampling a new recipe dish in family, sensed there might be more to the world than the great commonwealth of Reuben & Style, beyond doubt the finest business in the British Isles and, one day, perhaps, in Europe: not a university degree – of course not! – but a thing or things that might release him from his restlessness, his thirst for product innovation, from the tyrant stock-checking lists.

"There's room, isn't there, Alan? I've now forgotten your precise margin on clothes . . ."

The room quivered. Nobody said anything. Then one of the young women experimented with a superior smile. For it was a fact, one of the very few facts among the myths of Reuben & Style's long history, that gross profit margins were not discussed in public. Not even with the City that, Alan kept forgetting, actually owned his company. And certainly not with a supplier. Yet, there was a sense – a suspicion, perhaps, to be scrupulous – at Marylebone Road and in the stores, that Alan had all but expressed at his first bickering press conference at the time of the 1986 Annual Results and that Jane had cruelly brought to light, that under Derek MacArtnay, the gross margin on both food and clothes had crept too high, the supermarkets had slid in and stolen business, the fashion retailers were competitive on price, kidswear had tanked.

"It ain't so fat, Jane, that it can lose eighteen per cent."

"Are you sure, Alan? Excuse me, everybody, for being so late."

The room relaxed and, for most of the people there, began to get down to business: but for two of its inhabitants, Jane Haddon and Alan Nixon, the business had been done. For Alan knew that, whatever his gross margin, a secret which he kept locked in his heart, Jane's was much, much smaller; and, at a dollar exchange rate of $1.95 to the pound sterling, her markets were overwhelmed with product from the Far East and the Sub-Continent, and she just might close Motherwell; and Alan, who liked to source at home, not out of commercial patriotism or because Simon, with his horror of fascism, had broken with all his Czech and German suppliers in 1936 and sought to nurture a domestic textile industry, but because home suppliers could respond much more quickly than foreign to sudden demands in high-fashion items such as ladies underwear (but, oh! for the days of Simon and Jack, when the line that failed in London one season could be sent to York for the next . . .)

So, while the young men and women pulled at the merchandise on the racks, spread lace knickers and briefs and hip-huggers, unpicked the stitching of satinette bras – while irrelevant thoughts kept coming into their heads and going out again, shooed away by professional pride – already Alan and Jane, who were beyond such thoughts (or almost, because sex is a strong affection, stronger than ambition or love of profit), Alan Nixon and Jane Haddon had come to an understanding that, of the eighteen per cent increase imposed by a spastic government on the price at retail, the public would bear nothing at all but it would be divided, let's say by fifteen percentage points to three, between Reuben & Style and Associated British Textiles, and that Motherwell would be fixed.

Did Jane Haddon dislike Alan Nixon? She thought he was a good businessman, a fair businessman, a good merchant, a worthy successor to Simon and Jack and Harry and Derek, all good businessmen and great merchants. She also found Alan, though he would never know this, because he'd never been to school or travelled the world except to visit shops and knock off their merchandise, intensely interesting. This room with its plundered underwear was to her more magical than to have seen Pretty Meg Bellarmine in a dream; and, of all the things she could have done with her precious life, to be responsible, at the age of about thirty, a mere girl, for the remains of the United Kingdom's clothing industry, was the most romantic. But this secret Jane kept locked, as securely as Alan Nixon his sixty-seven per cent gross profit margin, in her heart.

Swaying up in the lift to her flat, which was in an apartment block called the Bagatelle in Arlington Street, W1, Jane said out loud: "Thank you, Stephen Cohen."

The flat was big and, because land in that part of London in those days was valuable, showy in the extreme. Jane had bought it with Johnny, just before their marriage, and kept it at their divorce. It was a memento of that short era, like her clothes, as if all Jane's predilections had been extinguished with her marriage. It was also deliriously expensive to keep but Jane, though she was paid relatively little – two hundred and ninety-three thousand pounds a year, according to a note to the 1986 Textiles accounts – could afford it. She had few other expenses.

She turned on the table lamps, one by one. Their concentrated light broke the room into pieces, mitigated its scale and ostentation. She poured herself a highball-glass of rum and picked up the telephone, replaced it, then picked it up again. She addressed her secretary's answering machine with the courtesy she used to that young man himself. She said, "Pete, it's Jane here, calling on Friday evening. Could you do me a favour and, the first thing you do this morning, call a member's agent at Lloyd's called Turpe, that's T-U-R-P-E, the senior partner's name is R.W. Turpe, I think that's Roderick or Roddie; and ask him for an appointment as soon as possible. It should take about an hour, and half an hour each side on the tube. Any day. Thank you, Pete. Hope you had a good weekend."

The usual Friday evening sounds frightened her, as if she were in a fever. The weekend stretched ahead, empty of social detail. Jane poured herself more rum. She wanted to get drunk. She wanted to make love. She thought: . . . I'm not going to tell you what she thought.

When Tolstoy began *Anna Karenina* with the proposition that all happy families are like one another, and each unhappy family unhappy in its own way, I don't think he was prattling. He was saying, I think, that happy families have no interest for novelists, who need change for their narratives, or at least change more easily communicable than the slow ageing of contented men and women; and that there are varieties of unhappiness, whereas happiness is a seldom condition, a sort of attunement of circumstances, which bears the same relation to unhappiness as a musical note to noise. I think he was saying that an unhappy marriage can be an inferno.

Neither Johnny nor Candida Bellarmine thought themselves unhappy. They got up together; breakfasted, lunched and dined together; went on walks and holidays together; read the same books and watched television together; slept together. They were faithful to each other, or at least I'm sure Johnny was faithful to Candida. Their neighbours thought them just the handsomest, luckiest couple around. Neighbours are a slow lot.

If it were possible to embody a person's affections, then Johnny carried on his back an excrescence, like the burden each pilgrim carries in illustrated editions of *The Pilgrim's Progress*. This burden, which caused him mentally to stoop a little or pause before climbing stairs or straighten before entering an occupied room, represented his first marriage: not necessarily a resentment of Jane or regret for her person or temperament but a sense of his own failure: that he had married and then, fourteen months later, divorced. The stoop, though evident to his friends and acquaintances only as a phantom or vestige, added greatly to his charm; and perhaps induced him to treat his second wife with especial gentleness, to hear her out on any topic she raised, to push in her chair at table and turn out her bedside light when she fell asleep over a magazine, to make love when he didn't want to and to think of other things when she didn't.

Candida Bellarmine also walked with a stoop, though it was more pronounced. She was younger than Johnny, by almost half a generation, and lacked his curiosity and scruple: she'd grown up, not in the tumult of the 1960s, but in the hard grind of the late 1970s, under the humiliations of the last Labour government and the revenge, in its Tory successor, of a bourgeoisie driven beyond distraction. She'd married the man she'd selected, had informed herself about his family and possessions, managed a famous house, a flower- and kitchen-garden, to the approbation of all who knew Johnny Bellarmine and some who didn't.

It was agreed by all that it was a damned good thing that Johnny had fired that chippy Jane Haddon and married Candida, who was perhaps a little *conventional* but was up to looking after the house. When Jane was there, said an interior decorator who lived at weekends in the lodge of a neighbour's park, there simply weren't any flowers in the house and I said to Jane: Dearest, you really must have some flowers and as for the Hawksmoor library, it's probably the greatest room in Europe, done well, and she painted it a sort of a coalite grey . . . and . . . and . . . All were agreed that what Wexley Park needed, what Johnny needed, what all the men of England needed, was a Sloane.

But Sloanes have hearts, as we all do; and Candida had begun to suspect, if not yet to articulate, that her family's social ambition and the hierarchies of English life had brought her not to comfort and respect but to a sort of prison; that she, too, would age and shed her looks, her body would become disagreeable to her and both fashion and happiness – or rather what she called fun – would have passed her by; that she, in short, had been sold a pup. Unlike Johnny, she displayed symptoms of her distress: a valetudinarianism that tested and mocked her husband's attention, and a craving for company.

Which last is why, on the evening of the day of the buyers' conference at Reuben & Style, at the very moment Jane was gaping over Green Park, twelve people separated husband and wife at the dinner table at Wexley Park; though Johnny sometimes smiled at her through the greenhouse flowers and the candle-light and the criss-crossed shop talk of the men down twenty feet of Hepplewhite, till she rose with an exaggerated swish of her dress, the men looked sadly into their wine glasses, then stood up and followed her out.

Stephen found country-house parties exhausting. He seemed to be always explaining himself. There was just so much conversation. There was conversation at breakfast and over the newspapers; before lunch and at lunch and after lunch; in the garden at mid-afternoon; at tea; and before dinner and during dinner and after dinner. He accepted such invitations, or rather Lizzie accepted them, because they had nothing better to do between Friday evening and Monday morning; and because Johnny was his friend, had assumed that title twenty years earlier at school and so inalienably that, even had he been a molester of children, he would never lose it.

None the less, Stephen needed respite. The talk over the fruit, between the men, had been of boot-polish: precisely, its fatal tendency to dry and crack into friable and useless pieces. It was as if all capital questions of society and political economy had been settled once and for all, leaving just these niggling relics of a once universal disorder. Deep in the sofas, the women exchanged the closest intimacies: Stephen found the conversation of women among themselves shameless, and hated to overhear it. He took his little coffee cup and littler spoon into an uninhabited corner of the drawing room, where he was shielded from company by the bulk of the politician Tom Burke and the boom and hiss of his pronouncements; but barely had he established himself, when he saw that thug from Lloyd's – Turpe, was it? Robert or Roger? Candida's uncle or something? – stepping towards him on embroidered carpet slippers and saying, to a point above Stephen's head:

"Know anything about the daubs, old boy?"

Stephen turned and looked at the square of canvas and oil paint in question. He did know. Because Jane had told him, in the days when it was Jane, standing with one arm under her bosom and the other holding a cigarette in air; and though he didn't remember the words exactly, I have looked them up in the *Voyages*. The Pieces which break from the large Islands are more dangerous than the Islands themselves, the latter are generally seen at a sufficient distance to give time to steer clear of them, wheareas the others cannot be seen in the night or thick weather till they are under the Bows. Great as these dangers are, they are in some measure compencated by the very curious and romantick Views many of these Islands exhibit, in short the whole fills the mind with admiration and horror, the first is occasioned by the beautifullniss of the View and the latter by the danger attending it, for was a ship to fall aboard one of these large pieces of Ice she would be dashed to pieces in a moment.

"I'm afraid not. You'll have to ask Candy." Having grown up without family possessions, Stephen was reluctant to speak of those of others; and anyway Turpe was the sort of fellow who saw not paint but congealed money.

"The curious thing," said Edward Wallow, who was chairman of Sotheby's or Christie's and now injected himself into their group, "is that he'd never actually seen an Antarctic iceberg. Actually, I don't think anybody in England at that time had seen such a thing, except Johnny and his men. He makes rather a fist of it though, don't you think?"

The repetitions of the pronoun *he* were a torment to Turpe, but he was bound by convention not to enquire more directly.

"Who's the painter?" asked Stephen, who took pity on him.

"Thomas Daniell, you prat," said Candida pleasantly. She took Wallow by his velvet arm and said: "Do help me, Edward." They turned and moved away smartly, as if to extinguish a small social fire.

"Do you know Eddy Durham's at Ingoldsby?" Turpe had recovered.

It would be better, thought Stephen, if this really were the eighteenth-century and these men true eighteenth-century parasites, eating Johnny's meat and drinking his drink and screwing his house-maids; instead of this commercial parasitism, where business is mere handmaid to snobbery, as if these men had selected their professions merely to be near Johnny and his type; or, more probably, as if commerce and snobbery were so implicated that they couldn't be unravelled. As he thought this, and as Johnny approached them with a bottle of antique brandy and two tiny glasses, Stephen realised he was suddenly out of date: that something had changed in the last months or even weeks, that there was about these people an independence: as if the prosperity of recent years – the boom in stocks and bonds, real property, pictures, furniture and taffeta curtain swags – had somehow emancipated them from their snobbish deference; that they no longer needed Johnny and his class as social authority and the long reign of the English nobility, which had survived the Reform Bill and the Repeal of the Corn Laws, wars, depression, penal taxes and much drink and gear, was now hurrying to its end. But at that moment, as Stephen, ravished by magnanimity and detachment – a Colbert, say, haunting the Sun King's entertainments *avec visage sombre et sévère* – a bourgeois phantom mouthing doom to nobility and monarchy – at that moment, Stephen saw that it was all balls: that at the core of his friend's existence was a hard nugget of commerce, polished no doubt by use and gilded by time, but commerce all the same; and that maybe history had not pronounced its last word on the Bellarmines.

"Mortgage the cat!"

Stephen had forgotten about Turpe. He looked at Lizzie, seated at the left of a head-high fireplace, knitting. She was short-sighted, but too vain to wear glasses and too lazy for lenses. He realised he felt affectionate towards her. He said, though not to R.W. Turpe: A couple of years from now, I'll dream about you, Lizzie, about your bust and little feet and creamy skin and be baffled that I ever let you go.

If all bedrooms were chapels to Lizzie Pinto, the Huahine Bedroom at Wexley Park was her cathedral. Beneath the distant ceiling, painted with a suggestive allegory, amid the little French furniture and old Chinese wallpaper, her folded clothes and scents and brushes and hat-boxes and bagged-up shoes and tissue-paper seemed not just items of women's fashion but the permanent essence of femininity; and revealed their true purpose, as some perplexing moves in the middle game at chess become explicable, no, necessary, at the moment of resignation. When she undressed, Lizzie had the unusual habit of taking off all of her top, or all of her bottom, at once, a practice which never left Stephen unaffected.

"Let's screw, babe," he said.

Which they did, but not before Lizzie had managed a question.

"What was that wine he gave you at dinner?"

"The Lafleur of 1961, I think she said."

"Cor! And he never touches it! Poor Johnny."

"But generous," said Stephen, and for years afterwards the word evoked for him the touch and shape and taste of Lizzie's bosom.

Sex restored the ancient relations of power in their love affair. At such moments, Stephen remembered what in her had entranced him: not just her femininity, and what she did with it, but her ignorance of all the inhibitions of his education. She'd once said, at the time when he was more eloquent in his attentions, "Upper-class girls aren't interested in talk, they just like their . . ." and indicated, in a general sort of way, what such persons liked. There was nothing in life she would not sample; and nothing she could not do without, except – and Stephen turned his head a fraction – a glass of water by her bed at night.

Later, but not much later, she said: "Cecilia Turpe says everybody's getting into Lloyd's. Shouldn't we, I mean I . . ." She lost her nerve.

Stephen turned her round, and pulled her into the bend made by his legs and belly. He thought: If Lizzie wants to write insurance, then there is absolutely and literally nobody still to come, and the market will crash. "No," he said.

Lizzie used her blockbuster. "You know Candy's screwing that awful man from Sotheby's."

He turned and looked up at the pink dome high above the bed. "Poor Johnny."

"Poor Katie Wallow!"

A bit later, half-engulfed with sleep, Lizzie said: "He hasn't got over Jane, has he?"

"What crap, Lizzie."

When Johnny Bellarmine was married for the second time, in the summer of 1983, his bride's family gave a party for them at the Reform

Club in Pall Mall. Stephen attended this party, because he had nothing better to do, and because he liked weddings. He liked to see the changes in his friends from school and university, changes of economic circumstance and physical condition, revealed at these three- or four-year intervals, as if in a social strobe-light. His observations, delivered on tides of champagne, filled him with a pleasant melancholy which he mistook for wisdom.

It was a hot day. Candida Turpe looked a picture. Her uncle made a long speech, mentioning the names of minor politicians. Somebody made some dirty jokes. A good champagne came round and round and round. Johnny's old female relations sat, furious and unattended, on little gilded chairs. Johnny looked over the moon.

Making his way, in no particular hurry, to the head of the stairs and the street, Stephen saw a pretty woman in a hat and a smart but not new yellow suit. She had thick black hair and the faint look of wounded surprise of all the Johnny-side guests: as the Olympian Gods must now look, deprived of the smoke of sacrifice. Stephen said to her: "I met you once, in Cyprus, in 1969, when you were on your honeymoon."

Her face opened like a bud in spring.

Stephen first saw Lizzie in the spring of 1969, the year his parents divorced, at a place west of Kyrenia called Apsos. He'd arrived at night; but after breakfast the next morning, as he walked down behind Mr Smith and Vijay Subota, he saw a round bay of transparent sea and two men in shorts working a cement-mixer. In the mouth of the bay was an island, on which a young man with fair hair and bad sunburn sat with his head on his knees. Swimming towards him, rising and falling on a strong crawl, was a slim girl in a flowered honeymoon bikini.

It was too far for Stephen to swim but not for Vijay, who swam for the school and Karnataka State; and Stephen saw, in the hot distance, gestures of pleasure and faint social recognition. As Vijay came out of the water back on Stephen's side, he said: "He's Rupert Cosby . . ."

"Heavens," said Mr Smith. "The stupidest boy I ever taught."

" . . . and she's Bellarmine's cousin."

Stephen was fourteen. Before that morning, he had never kissed a woman, seen the Mediterranean, eaten okra, mullet or garlic, or watched a cicada shed its wings or legs; but he could read Longinus *On the Sublime* without a dictionary. I think his parents' divorce had exacerbated the sense of self-exposure that was inseparable from life at a boys' boarding-school of that era. A sociable boy in Lewisham and at Pagham Head, he'd looked into a mirror and seen an asthmatic deity in a suit of early nineteenth-century mourning. I know that somewhere and at some moment – perhaps this very morning – he'd decided he'd do his A-levels and then be shot of it all – Mr Smith walking naked from the bathroom, Vijay oiling his shoulders, all the faint and Hellenic homosexuality – and spend his life in the company of women: a project he had followed with the utmost consequence, beginning on the beach at Apsos as Bellarmine's cousin stood slim and dripping in the sunshine.

"I thought, Rupert, that I could at least escape you here."

"Oh well, sir, I reckoned I needed some remedial Greek. This is my wife, Lizzie."

Mr Smith stood up. As Stephen shook her hand, he saw she was quite baffled; that she was not intelligent; and it would not be easy to make an impression on her.

"You're a terribly good swimmer."

"Oh! Not really."

"Well, Rupert and Lizzie, since we are all lodged in the same half-built hotel, we should perhaps have dinner together one evening."

"That would be lovely, sir."

"Martin."

"In that funny hotel! With Mr Smith and that Indian boy! Oh, it was so long ago! I was seventeen,* if you can imagine it!"

In the party noise, the prowling of photographers, the restlessness of small celebrities, I imagine they made a sort of clearing: a space made

* Eighteen

not so much by her social relief (though that obviously played a role) but by an intense and reciprocal sexual desire. Then Lizzie lost her poise – she must often have been put down in her life – and said to her excellent shoes:

"You've got a good memory for names."

"No, Lizzie, I recognised you."

It didn't seem to Stephen, in the tumult between them – which pained him, sharply, in his guts and groin – that that was flattery: all that was behind them, or in the future. Stephen stared at her eyes, just to see her happiness. She was, beyond any doubt, the happiest person in that room; and, not certainly but very probably, also at the reception for the Institute of Directors across the big landing.

"Mr Smith was incredibly helpful about Dick. But he just wasn't bright enough, poor boy. He's fantastically happy at Blosham's. It's a jolly good school."

Lizzie dear, public schools don't matter any more. "Is your husband here?"

"Oh, that all sort of came to an end. Still, we're the best of friends . . ."

"I'm sorry, Lizzie."

" . . . I saw him and Penny just last week."

Stephen decided that interrupting her was not a good idea.

"Then I sort of ran around with –" She mentioned the name of a mythic Irish film actor. In terms of confidences, they might have been in a bed.

"That was brave." Again, he'd interrupted some formal *curriculum vitae*.

". . . but it just became, you know, rather trying." She tipped her hand to suggest, with that tiny gesture, the seas of drink in which O'Hara nightly bathed; but the hand drew Stephen to her Chanel coat and skirt, a relic of those long evenings in Bel Air.

"I have to go now, Lizzie. Let me kiss you goodbye."

He felt, as he touched her cheek, her heart flutter in her ribs. Then he went down the stairs, thinking how loathsome it was to be a man in his prime.

I don't know what happened next, because I can't be everywhere. I imagine a postcard, in a good woman's handwriting, and embedded in some useless information, beside the final reminiscence of Cyprus, a telephone number; which becomes a house in a divorced district of London (Chiswick, Clapham), an afternoon, a door opening at the end of a small front-garden; and Lizzie Pinto's face a little flushed, not from excitement but from tidying the kitchen, setting out the tea things and also whisky, or whatever O'Hara had had; but they kiss in the stained-glass hall sunlight, because words aren't going to help; and in her bedroom, which is papered yellow, past the swags and tucks and polish of her dressing-table, the eighteenth-century drawings, the furniture marooned from country houses, the scent of Arpège, they touch and kiss again – a man and a woman who've made a lot of love, done little else – unhitch his tie, unpeel her best underwear, mesmerised by each other's familiarity; and from this chance meeting, stumble through stages of faltering intimacy, friends and accomplices, towards a beckoning future: which is a boy sitting in his shirt on a beach, and a girl cleaving the Mediterranean.

2

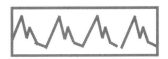

The building that once housed the insurance market known as Lloyd's of London was erected in the first years of the 1980s at a cost of one hundred and eighty-five million pounds, and countless injuries; the gravest of those, as it turns out, down the same elevator shaft up which Jane was now riding, rapidly, and suicidal with vertigo.

The elevator, which ran up the outside of the building in homage to a hotel Mr Turpe had once stayed in for a convention in Atlanta, Georgia, gave no clue, in its whimsy and bravado, to the function of the building that it served; nor, for that matter, did the men riding up with Jane, leaning in their suits against blue sky, staring insolently at her legs. By the time Jane was shown into the boardroom, she was in a fury of disapproval.

"Lady Bellarmine!" said Roddie Turpe, striding across acres of carpet towards her. "I was just saying, at the weekend, at . . ."

"I believe, Mr Turpe, that as I'm divorced from Johnny Bellarmine, I don't need his name."

Turpe stopped and teetered, as if he'd collided with some obstacle three feet in front of her. "Okedoke," he boomed. "Miss Haddon. Or is it Ms?"

"Whichever you prefer," said Jane, viciously, and sat down at the long boardroom table.

Tricky, thought Turpe. Chippy, thought Turpe. Rich, thought Turpe. Jane's telephone message, conveyed with certain secretarial nuances uninterpretable to me by Pete to Mr Turpe's secretary, had been waiting for the great man that Monday morning, when, dreary with Wexley Park kümmel and his own anxiety, he entered the high portals of Lime Street. Not wishing to appear eager, he had had his secretary offer Pete that Thursday.

"I imagine you know the ropes, Mrs Haddon," he said. "I wouldn't presume to lecture you about insurance. Some of the external Names we've had here, particularly in the last couple of years, have had to be walked through and . . ."

"Actually, I am entirely ignorant of insurance," said Jane. Stop it, she thought . . . Smile.

Jane smiled. "I'm afraid I have no feeling for the risks and rewards of underwriting at Lloyd's," she said.

"We're looking," said Turpe, lurching into his rigmarole, "for a return to Names of ten per cent of stamp a year over the insurance cycle. Since the Council's solvency ratio is at present thirty per cent and you should be able to achieve up to ten per cent on the funds you deposit with us, we would hope to gain for you a return before tax of somewhat over forty per cent a year. I won't make you a fortune, Mrs Haddon, but I won't lose you one either. I wouldn't want you mortgaging the cat."

You're a fool, Turpe, thought Jane, or a crook. A safe investment yields three per cent a year. An annual return of forty per cent must, by definition, carry unspeakable risks.

But these thoughts Jane kept to herself. She said: "So. If I deposited £30,000 or a bit more with you, I could write £100,000 in insurance premium and expect, over the peaks and troughs of the business, a return of £10,000 a year plus say £2,000 in interest on the deposited money, which is £12,000 or, I suppose, about forty per cent."

"As it were," said Turpe, a little uneasy.

"And is a line of £100,000 about usual? High? Low?"

Turpe panicked. He said: "Quite frankly, I do not advise my Names to underwrite at that level. First, the return is merely nominal. Second, you simply cannot get the spread of risk. I'd be looking to push you on to at least six of the best syndicates, if I can, preferably those under-written by Derek Maughan who is the only certified genius in this building, a wizard at the box. You really should meet him, you know, Mrs Haddon, see the Room and the brokers queuing up at his box, you'll enjoy it. That would be, say, 46, 311, 412, 518, 541 and 617. Marine, aviation, motor, LMX. If you do decide to retain Turpe & Maughan as your agents, I would have to advise a line of not less than one million and, ideally, a mill-plus. You know that you don't have to ante up for the solvency? We'll arrange a bank guarantee on Arlington Street."

Get out of my life, will you? Jane felt obscurely polluted, as if her flat had been burgled. She waved her hand, as if to say: Let's leave the precise level of my premium exposure for the moment. She said: "Remind me, will you, please, what LMX is?"

Cunt. "London Market Excess of Loss," Turpe said, which did not answer Jane's question, let alone yours. "Look, I think I'd really like to get you together with Derek. He more or less invented that market. He's not much of a charmer, and definitely not one of us, but I think for somebody with your experience in business . . ." He strode to the boardroom door. "A fox at the box, Mrs Haddon."

To her great relief, Jane descended by escalator, which came down in pettifogging zig-zags towards a vast floor open to the building's roof. As she came nearer, the people and things took on definition like a city from an aircraft on landing. Jane was shown round by Turpe and an usher. She saw the Lutine Bell, the red-liveried waiters, the Council room taken piece by piece from some demolished country house: elements of the past preserved in this palace of glass and titanium, as if to say: This is what we did, old girl, three hundred years and never a claim not paid. And what do we do now, well, it's rather brainy and a bit complicated, don't you worry your pretty pussy about that now. Enjoy yourself.

When Jane started in business, investigating the United States Mid-West for businesses for the Doncaster Group, if she found so much as a picture in the boardroom in Akron or Kalamazoo – forget 707s or fishing-camps on the Restigouche! – James Doncaster would reduce his offer. She tried to imagine the phantom estate supporting this vast pleasure dome, tried to conjure flaking freighters on mercury seas, satellites in the night sky, ethylene crackers in the boondocks; but her imagination, never strong, failed her. There were no women about, which unnerved her.

"Derek!" shouted Turpe, burrowing through the gossiping brokers.

A man looked sharply up from a computer terminal. He looked unwell. Wet eyes skipped over Turpe and landed on Jane. "Who the fuck are you?"

"Jane Haddon."

"The knickers girl?"

A clerk tittered.

"The same."

"What do you want?"

"To know about LMX."

"Well, you have a catastrophe risk and you lay it off – what we call re-insure – in layers. I saved this bloody market when Alicia hit in 1983. If you don't get a hurricane, you make a fucking pile of money. Anything else?"

"What happens if you have more than one catastrophe?"

Derek Maughan looked at her for a second time. "We've never had more than one a year. You're talking about, OK, a hurricane in southern Florida, a big marine loss, say an oil-platform in the North Sea or a lost VLCC, refinery fire, rag-head war, all in the same year. If you're worried about all that, I'd stick to panties."

"Thank you, Mr Maughan," said Jane.

"Bit of a rough customer," said Turpe, happily, as they descended to the street.

"But a fox at the box."

On the tube back to Oxford Circus, Jane buried her head in the *Financial Times*. Dreary headings and a close-up photograph of Margaret Thatcher dissolved before her. She cried not because of Derek Maughan's rudeness – which, if anything, pleased her, as confirming adamantine prejudices – but out of rage. She thought what she thought to the numb and plutocratic plane-trees of Green Park that past Friday night, after the buyers' meeting at Reuben & Style, and I was too stingy to reveal. She thought: Now, I have you, my boy.

She also thought, for a moment, of riding on home, for it was past five.

But it was noon in New York. And anyway, a woman's work is never done.

Lord Doncaster – Jimmy to the financial press but nobody else – Jane's chairman, mentor and, it was universally assumed, lover, lived for much of the year in New York, in a large apartment on Park Avenue in the 60s. James Doncaster did not like the United States and, for precisely eighty-nine days of the year, passed his time in the gambling hells of Berkeley Square and the racecourses of Surrey that he had loved in his youth. Like many exiles, he still carried about him the atmosphere of the period of his expatriation, which was 1973, the year of the Barber Boom and Aspinall's and a little bother with the Revenue. On his dining-table in the Park Avenue apartment, he kept and promiscuously offered to astonished guests a bottle of H.P. Sauce which was made by a company he said – wrongly, as it turns out – he owned.

But despite the innuendoes of the *Lex* column and the sniggers of the City, Doncaster had never so much as kissed Jane and did not even fancy her. After her interview, which took place in the autumn of 1982, he'd taken her out to dinner at the Cenci, a restaurant on 61st and Lexington which was his favourite, and her eagerness and severity repelled him. On the pavement, before the idling limousine, she'd said: "I'll sleep with you if that's what you want, but I don't advise it." He hired her because she was English, or rather Scots, and because she had an idea. What that idea was, I don't know or much care: I think it was that there was liquidation value in very, very large corporations in disreputable industries, such as tobacco or waste management. All that mattered was that Jane had an idea and Lord Doncaster, after thirty-five years in business, had none.

In 1982, the Doncaster Group owned thirty-one textiles factories in England, Scotland and Northern Ireland, manufacturing Donelle rayon and artificial silks, nylon under a process licensed from Du Pont, acetate yarn and cigarette tow and several proprietary acrylic and polyester fibres; and twelve clothing factories making bed-sheets, blankets, ladies hose and underwear, shirtings and rainwear. These businesses, that had come attached to the acquisitions of Debex in 1977 and Spandron in 1979 and been left as the residue of their liquidations, like ash in a Petri dish, made small profits or small losses depending on the dollar exchange rate. (Because manufacturers in the Far East priced their goods in dollars, a fall in value of that currency and a corresponding rise in sterling, made their products irresistible to Oxford Street; and *vice versa*.)

Doncaster had not entered a factory since accompanying his blind grandfather round a brickworks in Bedfordshire at the age of fifteen; for he was shy and lazy, and did not want to see the human warp of his business lest it affect his judgement. He had forgotten about these assets until Jane sent him, from a Holiday Inn in Canton, Ohio, a short paper on the subject eight months after her employment.

"Forget it, girl," said Doncaster at Sandown Races ten days later.

Jane bit her lip. Doncaster, whose glacially slow racemare Radio Girl had just come fourth in a plater, thought: I'm in a fucking rut.

"How much do you want?"

"We need to spend four times depreciation, plus in-filling of product lines, closing all primary capacity with redundancy and severance. Three hundred million pounds over five years discounted to present value at a rate of four per cent."

"She's gone mad. Already."

It was Lord Doncaster's invariable practice, when presented with invoices from Wall Street investment bankers and lawyers for advice given and counsel tendered, to divide the sum by three and pay it by return. He had not, up to that point, been sued which made him feel he was a clever fellow: in reality, of course, Cold Revett Spear and Maedel, Berliner merely billed three times their hours, as Jane very well knew. He now said, in the Doncaster Group box, at Sandown Races:

"You can have £100 million over seven years. And don't blub."

In the ladies of the members' enclosure, Jane swallowed a handful of Tums, an American antacid that was the most enduring memento of her United States residence. She had an unremitting pain in her stomach which, more than anything, defined for her the first half of the decade of the 1980s. During that period, the Doncaster Group perplexed its followers in the City and the financial press by unexpected and contradictory mutations: in reality, the business was being bent and moulded to accommodate Jane's vertical ascent. In 1985, Doncaster announced that the group would be split into two parts, each with its own stock-market quotation, and consisting of a clothing business employing seventy thousand people at sixteen manufacturing sites to be known as Associated British Textiles (with Jane as managing director); and the remainder, the good bits, the expanding bits, the profitable bits, the fun bits, and all the US bits, to be managed in the old way by James Doncaster.

The idea had been Jane's but the detailed work was done by Stephen Cohen of the merchant bank S.L. Brimberg, for a fee of twenty-eight million pounds which transformed his standing at that firm; but Stephen was not able to prevent Lord Doncaster from taking two billion pounds in cash out of Textiles, which had to be financed by bank loans secured on the industrial plant; for Doncaster was a mean sod. Jane passed out of the business pages and into *Vogue*, which welcomed her back without comment, as if her absence for five years had been an oversight; but though she succeeded in refinancing the loans, at somewhat lower rates of interest and longer maturities in the European debt markets, her pains returned and with them an implacable insomnia.

Which brings us to the present Thursday evening, the telephone ringing at Burlington Street and Pete over the intercom: "Himself?"

"James," she said.

"Hey, girl, get your arse over here." The telephone connexion, which originated in a mobile phone in a limousine stuck in mid-town traffic, was bad. "Wall Street's going to go, and I mean go, tomorrow or Monday. I'm doing a suite at the Pierre, some booze and a Quotron, Charlie Lauriston and a few lads, it'll be fun! Hell, Jane, I had lunch with Charlie and Gordo White at Cenci and this waiter came up, some Albanian or something, and said: Sir Lauriston, do you like Microsoft at 80? This market is going to tank."

Lord Doncaster was an impressionable man, as good business people generally are; and Sir Charles Lauriston was, in those days, a commanding personality.

"Are you short, James?"

A short seller sells shares he does not own in the expectation that the stock market will fall and that, when the time comes to deliver these shares to the buyer – ten days under the rules of the New York Stock Exchange – he can buy them more cheaply in the market and make a profit.

"Do bears shit in the woods?" Then he shrieked: "Jesus, Jane, did you see that? These black despatch guys . . ."

"I'm in London, James."

"So get on the bird."

The invitation, Jane knew, was not sincere. She also knew she would be out of place at this elderly bears' party, amid the champagne and contraband cigars, the extravagant wagers – Charlie's timberlands to Gordo's Nevada gold mines – the arithmetical blondes. Adopting her chairman's Americanisms, she said: "I'll take a rain check."

"Look, Jane, I'm serious." Her coldness always infuriated him. He said: "The dollar's going to crash and there'll be the mother and father of a deflation. You're going to push out your debt . . ."

"Suck eggs, James."

". . . no, listen, I'm still chairman of your little sewing-shop. No capital investment at all for eighteen months. And close bloody Motherwell."

"I will not close Motherwell."

"You're fired," said Lord Doncaster, and then: "Joke!" He rang off.

Jane walked out of her office and into the reception room and leaned with a hand on Pete's desk. She said: "Will you book me on the Glasgow shuttle for tomorrow, up on the 8.15, down on the 19.30. Two seats, please, Pete."

"Sure," said Pete, and raised his eyebrows.

"Joe! A moment, if you have it."

Joe was Joe Morris, the finance director of Associated British Textiles, and the only other head office functionary: Jane was much praised for her delayering of management though, in reality, she'd arrived at Textiles to find no central staff at all and had added three (including herself). Domesticity, even of the public office, was not her virtue.

"Steve Cohen's just been on," said Joe. "The big piece has been underwritten, and, wait for it, at a sixteenth over."

This intelligence, reporting as it did that the main and most intractable portion of Textiles' debt had been converted into a security and sold to a group of banks at a rate of interest just one-sixteenth ($^{1}/_{16}$th) of a percentage point above the wholesale price of money in the London market, would, in normal circumstances, have been worth to Jane at least two bottles of Tums. Instead, she said:

"Will you come up with me to Motherwell?"

Joe was a good accountant, but he kept his distance from Jane. Blessed by a paradisiacal upbringing in Muswell Hill, he thought of women as mothers, lovers, servants – or, to be quite accurate, just as mothers; and he sensed something disordered in Jane's nature and position. "Do you need me?"

"No, Joe, I do not need you. I'll go on my own."

Jane went back into her office and telephoned Stephen at Brimberg's.

"Well, get him out of that meeting," she said, and then collected herself. "It's Jane Haddon. Excuse me for being so abrupt."

"Hi there, cross-patch," said Stephen, evidently speaking from a vacated conference room. "Don't you just love me?"

"Would you please meet me at Heathrow tomorrow in good time for the 8.15 Glasgow shuttle?"

"Will you sleep with me, if I do?"

Not vacated.

"If necessary."

"I'll have to cancel a lunch."

"There'll be lunch in the canteen," said Jane obtusely.

"Hey, you're finally going to shut that rust-bucket at last!"

Jane said nothing.

"You're really going to shut that thing down, Jane?"

"No, Stephen, I don't think so."

33

3

The Queen Elizabeth Textile Works in Motherwell, which was opened in 1962, occupies an entire city block on the A8, the dual-carriageway from Glasgow to Edinburgh. Its stone pediment and colonnaded wings suggest an architectural era anterior to its construction and a confidence its builders may not have felt. It was sited in Motherwell as a favour to the then Prime Minister, Harold Macmillan, who shamelessly pushed and cajoled Lord Glass of ICI towards this part of Scotland so as to mop up the labour made suddenly redundant by the sealing of the deep Lanark coal-pits and the short orders on the Clyde. That the plant would, in the course of time, employ only women and thus transform the patrimonial relations within the working families of East Lanark did not occur to anybody as significant. Lord Glass himself preferred a site outside Derry in Ulster, but let himself be persuaded. They did things differently in those days.

If Lord Glass had a plan, it was this: that wages would fall to a point at which the outlying regions of the British Isles could be converted once again into great centres of manufacturing to rival the mills of Japan. He had visited Japan, both as an officer attached to MacArthur's staff and later to discuss the building of a joint-venture ethylene plant, and was impressed to his heels; but nobody, least of all Glass, could have seen that these same Japanese, as their living standards rose from the abyss of war and nuclear holocaust, would themselves abandon textile-weaving for automobiles and consumer electronics; and their orphaned mills be dismantled and re-assembled elsewhere in Asia where wages were yet lower: in Korea and Hong Kong, and then Thailand, India and mainland China.

Meanwhile, Motherwell, with its sixteen hundred women and its great looped dyeing and finishing lines, never turned a profit in all its history. A capital investment plan, sent up to the main board of ICI in 1975 but never discussed, passed out of all possibility with the sale of the plant by Lord Reardon to Debex the next year, and its eventual destination within the Doncaster Group. James Doncaster saw a source of cash in the depreciation of the machines and the mortgaging, and then sale and leaseback to an Edinburgh pension fund, of the ground site; with the effect that by October, 1987, the place was badly in need of paint, windows all over the upper storey were broken, the antique time-keeping machines kept failing, management was morose and slapdash while the workforce had fallen prey to a seedy radicalism. It was a miracle that boxer-shorts from Motherwell, and the most conventional ladies' briefs, still sold in thousands of pairs a day in Reuben & Style's great store on Oxford Street; but the question of product quality had come to lower over Jane's dealings with Alan Nixon – hung, like a third presence, in those meeting rooms high over the Marylebone Road – a question she'd been curiously reluctant, for a woman so decisive, to address. It was as if this forlorn place – the flaking gates on the Lanark Road, the howling rain, the Trot girl in the charity-shop leather coat pressing *Workers Week* on the jostling night shift – had disabled her.

"Don't try it, Jane," said Stephen in wonder. "They'll crucify you."

In the back seat of the company Escort, Jane seemed to shrink into a corner, sealed by rain.

The meeting Jane had called, for the combined shifts, took place in the relief canteen, a long low-ceilinged room in the basement. It was so packed nobody could sit, and Jane simply jumped on to a red plastic chair and started speaking. Stephen, marooned among the overalled women in his City pin-stripe – a costume which he sensed Jane hated him for – could see only her head.

"Good morning. My name is Jane Haddon and I am managing director of Associated British Textiles."

"Get on with it, lass!" shouted someone from the back, a noted wit on the No. 2 printing machine.

"I'll take your questions at the end, if you don't mind."

"Weren't no question," said the wag.

"Let her speak," someone else shouted; and, this finding approval with the women, Jane proceeded.

"I don't think you know but I was born in this town. My father was assistant works manager here when it was owned by ICI (Scotland). My mother was duty nurse on the night shift. No plant in the group means more to me, personally, or in the context of the business. I need you to understand this, ladies, before I go on."

Jane stopped talking. Stephen, lulled into infantile comfort by the presence of so many women, pulled himself together. He directed a thought at her: Don't take such risks, Jane. Don't take any risks.

Nobody said anything. Attagirl, thought Stephen.

"As you also know, this plant has never in its twenty-five years of operation provided its owners with anything recognisable as a profit. In recent years, it has been sustained by a general inflation of retail prices, which has allowed us to impose price increases on our customers. I do not believe this inflation will continue, but, on the contrary, there will be a depression in our main markets and static or even falling prices. I may be wrong on this. What is clear is that your chief customer, Reuben & Style, is no longer willing to take product from this factory because of its poor record for delivery and quality. I'm sorry, but you must let me speak. There will be ample time for questions after I have finished.

"What this means is that your product will now be sold in commodity markets where it will compete solely on price – let me repeat that, ladies, solely on price – with un-unionised, sweatshop labour, whether in Singapore or McClintock Road. I remain wholly committed to a unionised workforce and decent rates of pay and I cannot permit this factory to threaten the other plants. I have respon-sibilities to them, to our customers and our owners . . . Yes, call them bloody capitalists, but they have absolute power over your jobs and my job and Jim Wallace's. And I will close Motherwell, today if necessary, if it menaces the rest of the business. You should also be aware of that.

"Listen to me, please.

"When I became chief executive of this company in 1986, I knew already that Textiles' chief problem . . . its chief problem and also its chief opportunity lay in Motherwell. The problem has two parts. The first is defective investment, miserably inadequate investment, stretching back twenty-five years. Well, I'm glad we agree on something. Let's see if we can agree on something else. I saw then that the site needed the computer-controlled knitting machinery that was first promised to you in 1968, by ICI (Scotland) in 1975, and by Debex the next year; but I was hindered by the very high levels of debt and the mortgages taken out at the time of the demerger. I am now, and after discussion with Reuben & Style, prepared to authorise that line, which will represent a capital investment of sixty-five million pounds and will, I believe, secure the future of this site to the end of the century. It is by far the largest investment ever made at Motherwell since 1962, and one of the largest in Scotland for a generation."

Jane paused. Around her, there was silence. She continued:

"I am prepared to put a detailed proposal to the board of Textiles at its meeting on the twenty-third. I give you my word, and I have never broken my word in business or elsewhere. In return, I want you to do something for me, something very, very, very hard."

Jane stopped again. Stephen sensed, rather than saw, that she was beginning to tremble. Even so, he closed his eyes. He heard:

"I am asking each and every one of you to accept a cut in pay of twenty per cent to go into force with your next pay packets; and running . . . and running . . . and running . . . I'm sorry, but I cannot speak to you unless I have some quiet."

Stephen opened his eyes. The air was thick with hatred: as if the women, having long expected such a proposal from management, had trained to the limit for their response. He sensed rage and despair and also an unexpected sadness: that the QE Works, that might have been something in the world, was going to ground. Jane was looking round, helplessly. She did not have a big voice and hated to shout. She had lost control, and the essence of her life was control.

But Jane was a seldom individual – else why would I have invented her? What had she expected, applause? She called over the moving heads:

"Before I continue, I want you to hear Mr Cohen . . . Mr Cohen of the banking firm of S.L. Brimberg, who will outline to you much better than I can the company's additional offer to you. Mr Cohen's team . . ."

Stephen woke from his reverie, felt the women around him shrink from his masculinity and City suit, not in hostility but in a sort of exasperated patience. Before he grasped the scale of what Jane had done to him, a path had opened across the lino to the gallows chair. As he sprang up, he tried to catch Jane's eye, to get some inkling of what she wanted from him, but she had slipped back among the women, was staring at him, not angrily, but at the limit, too, of her patience. He thought perhaps he should take off his jacket and then remembered, blast, that he had on American braces, embroidered with a motif of bulls and bears.

"I think I should stand up here, too," he bawled and then adjusted his voice. He was beyond anger with Jane. Panic engulfed him. All the securities of his social class and sex had been stripped away. Jane had thrown him to the wolves of hers. His eyes fluttered to the windows, in their Sixties metal frames, slashed with rain. He heard a roaring, which must have been the wind outside. He was happy as he had never been in his life.

"Good afternoon, ladies. My name is Stephen Cohen and I am a partner of the London merchant bank S.L. Brimberg. What I want to propose to you today is preliminary and depends for its implementation not only on yourselves and the board of Associated British Textiles, but also on the approval of a special meeting of the company's shareholders and the Inland Revenue." OK, thought Stephen, everything on earth needs an EGM and the pigging Revenue, now what, sweety-pie? "When Miss Haddon first retained me on this matter, it was clear to me and the group I assembled, that Textiles could not ask these sacrifices of you, without very substantial compensation."

Now what, boy?

"What we're working on is some modality whereby, in return for the income you forego – the twenty per cent – you receive . . . Can everybody hear me, all right? . . . Is that better? . . . In return for your lost pay, you receive ownership participations in the company. In other words, you get to own your employer."

Hell! What do these women earn? How can I do this, if I don't know what they earn? Perhaps ask one of them, like at the panto? Look, it's got to be between £6,000 and £12,000 a year, just below the average wage. Jane! Did you say one-thirty a week? Jane! I hate you just so much.

"Let's assume a case, where one of you takes home a hundred pounds a week . . ."

Stephen looked into a woman's eyes, and they were stony.

"You're foregoing £20 a week over five years, which is twenty times fifty times five, which is £5,000. At the moment the pay agreement comes into effect, each of you will be issued with shares of a new class of Textiles stock, which will not be tradeable – can't be sold or bought – and will be blocked as to dividends. Since Textiles opened in the stock-market this morning at 98 pence, you'll receive about a thousand shares a year, or five thousand over the five years of the agreement. At the end of this period, the shares will be unblocked and the accumulated dividends – five years worth – paid over to you. And – and this, ladies, is the key to the deal and what I've sweated blood and candlelight over – these shares will no longer be worth 98 pence. We believe that because of the tremendous leap in productivity at this site, because of what is not so much a pay cut as a pay deferment, and because of the new automated line, these shares should be worth substantially more than 98 pence. One of our models produces a figure of 305 pence, one of 235 pence. There is a strong possibility that, in return for your sacrifice now, you could at Christmas of 1992 be in possession of a windfall of as much as £20,000 each, including dividends, and that for the most junior of you."

Stephen let this immense sum hang in the air for a moment. He looked at Jane, but she was staring at him with the same baffled suspicion as the women around her.

Then he said: "Let me add that though middle management will also receive stock in return for its sacrifices, head office will not be so compensated, as you would have heard if you'd allowed your managing director to finish. What I want to do is this. Jim Wallace now has the details of the proposal which will be typed up and posted round the plant, and you will therefore have the opportunity to discuss it with one another and your union representatives. On it will also be a phone number and either I or other members of my team will be available to answer all your questions at any reasonable time of day or night. I am also available if you wish me to come up again, and go through the proposal in smaller groups. I think that's all I have usefully to say at this stage, and I don't think there's anything to be gained by a discussion now. Miss Haddon and I have a plane to catch."

Stephen jumped off the chair, and the shock of the hard lino made his knees buckle in exhaustion and relief. Jane did not replace him, but simply said to a point above the women's heads: "These are quite intricate matters, and I'll return to discuss them further. Thank you very much for listening to me. Goodbye."

When Stephen finally made his way up to the main entrance-lobby, Jane was the centre of busy management attention.

"Edinburgh, too," she wailed.

"I'm afraid so, Jane," said a woman, evidently Jim Wallace's secretary. "But Manchester is still open."

Jane looked round wildly: it was as if the thought of spending any longer in this place was peril and shame to her, as if it were under heavy mortar fire and of no tactical value whatever. "Can I take a car, Jim? I've just got to get down."

"You can have the Cavalier, Jane."

The glass doors blew in rain, which sprang up off the forlorn car park with its handful of management saloons. Jim Wallace held up a golf umbrella and as Jane fought with her raincoat, she caught sight of Stephen. She clattered the length of the hall towards him, and extended her hand. She said: "How dare you lie to these women, Stephen? I will never use your firm or speak to you again."

"I didn't. Or not much. I can do it, Jane. Trust me."

She looked hard at his face, as if he were a stranger. It occurred to Stephen that trust was not one of Jane's mental attitudes. At length, she turned away. "Please call me at home tomorrow morning."

"What do you mean?" he hissed. "I'm coming with you. You think I'm staying the weekend in the Travellers Wee Rest in Motherwell! Let's go."

"But you're billing me," she said.

"The clock's off, Jane. Let's just go."

Jane shrugged. Stephen took the umbrella from Jim Wallace, who relinquished it, saying, "Take care, Jane, it's right windy out there," and they ran, bent double, through the surging film of water on the car park.

Jane believed she inhabited a private world, enclosed by a personality she thought intact. It did not occur to her, as she felt the rain wetting and cooling her skin, that she was watched from the basement window; or that the person watching her saw not a businesswoman and boss, created from uncounted triumphs and miseries, but to-die-for clothes and shag-me shoes, a bouncing umbrella, some rich geezer who really fancied her: in short, that person saw liberty and wanted it.

"Are you coming, girl?"

In the relief canteen doorway, two women in overalls leaned in postures of exasperation. This was how they expressed affection.

Cathy McKay turned from the window, and slouched towards them. She hated their kindness to her. She wasn't sure of much, but she was sure she wasn't going to spend her years stitching peach-coloured bras at the QE Works.

"So who's she?" she said.

The women rolled their eyes. "Tell you about her one day."

Jane drove. As they turned on to the A8, cars were plunging in vees of headlit spray on the far carriageway. She said: "How much do you charge, Stephen, as a matter of interest? I'd like to know."

"Brimberg's bill five hundred pounds an hour for partners."

"You whore," she said. "And pompous, too. Why do British men, as soon as they've got two feet on the ladder, get so fucking pompous? And while we're at it, how come you got so good at investment banking suddenly?"

These questions Stephen treated with the contempt they deserved. He said: "Jane, I went into business because you were there."

"PLEASE!" she said in a New York City accent. Then she said: "Thank you, thank you, thank you, thank you, thank you," in tones of diminishing sarcasm. "Thank you, Stephen," she said.

"I'm better without preparation. I'm sorry about your salary. It was just too good to miss."

"Can you really do it?"

"What? Cut your pay?"

Jane clicked her tongue against her teeth, a habit Stephen found intolerably provoking.

"Yes," he said. "Anything for you. Unless there's a depression. Can we hit the pension fund?"

"No," Jane shrieked. "James gave himself a bloody contributions holiday in 1983. The Revenue will be very hard, Stephen. Very hard. They loathe James."

"I can handle the Revenue. Look, Jane, do we have to talk about fucking business all the time." They were at a swimming roundabout.

"I have no other conversation." And: "It's a good plan, Stephen. I'm so grateful to you."

"You're welcome. Let's have a spliff."

"NO! Help me, Stephen. This is just awful. We need Dumfries."

Stephen peered into the horizontal rain, saw the word Lockerbie slide by in a smear of headlight.

"There. Left. Now."

Jane sat, bunched over the steering-wheel. She said: "They say it's getting hotter."

"What? What are you talking about?"

She glanced at him, then took a breath, as if rejecting the gambit as too taxing of his understanding. It was another habit Stephen found

43

exceedingly unlovely. "Look, Johnny is a rich man and can look after himself. If you want to help somebody, do something for the amateur Names at Lloyd's. Many of them aren't rich and don't know the risks they are running."

"What crap, Jane! They know perfectly well what they're doing. It beats working, that's all."

"They're all writing catastrophe insurance for tiny premiums, without having the faintest idea what risks they are insuring or how they should be priced. Even if the syndicates do book profits, they're siphoned off as management expenses by the insiders. I have never seen such an extravagant operation in my life. And they have this thing they call the Old Years' problem: vast claims on old pollution and workers' compensation policies, which were written in the Fifties and Sixties but where the damage is only just coming to light . . ."

"How the fuck did you find this out?"

Jane didn't answer the question. She said: "You could write to the *FT*, if you're that bothered about it. Or write to the Council of Lloyd's and send a copy to the *Financial Times*. And anybody else you choose."

"Jock Marshall won't publish it!"

"He will if I ask him to. Look, do you want me to write it? You just sign it?"

"Both of us, Jane."

"Oh, for God's sake!" And then: "All right."

"You'll never forgive Johnny, will you?"

Jane swerved horizontally on to the shoulder. "I can't do this, Stephen. I can't. I can't."

"What's happening to this country. It's like bloody Jamaica. I'll drive, OK, and you can crash for a bit. I'll wake you up at Manchester."

Stephen worked his way round the car, buffeted by wind and doused with truck spray, and, as he opened the driver's door, and saw Jane's wet legs disappearing into the back, he had an idea.

After fifteen miles, he said: "You never told me about your mum and dad."

"There're a lot of things I never told you about."

Jane woke to a stationary car, and to thunder, which was waves leaping at her over a sea-wall. To her, still drowned in sleep, they seemed in their fury like ferrets she'd once seen, tearing at the chicken-wire of their cage.

"Where are we?"

"Southport, Lancashire. A hotel called the Northern Star. I just couldn't hack it."

"Why did you bring us here, Stephen."

"For auld lang syne, Janet."

4

Even when he was at his lowest, Stephen Cohen never forgot that he'd seen Jane Bellarmine inject heroin into her wrist in a hotel bedroom in Southport, Lancashire in 1978 or 1979. He kept the picture by him, as someone keeps a beloved's photograph on his bedside table; or as another man remembers, at a time of frustration, that he has a beautiful wife or affectionate children or a job full of possibilities or a hundred thousand pounds in the stock market.

Stephen always remembered her as Jane Bellarmine: not, for example, as Jane or Jane Haddon or The Lady Bellarmine or Janet McKay which was the name she was given at birth or not long after. When he woke at four in the morning – it was always four, though he turned and blinked, pathetically, at his alarm clock – his mouth dry, his right side both numb and painful, and frightened, scared out of his wits – though of what, he didn't know – it was always Jane Bellarmine to whom he appealed: a name commonplace and exotic, a compound of city streets and white shores waving with copra palms, and comprehending the whole history of his country.

It was 1979, more or less, though for Stephen the years at the turn of the 1980s had a habit of running into one another for the purposes of recollection. He was lying on a sofa, feet up. At the back of his head, he sensed – for he'd seen them from the Esplanade – two windows, two balconies of white filigree cast iron, road, sea-wall, strip of sand and the sea turning over and over as far as Ireland, green as a fern by day, but now bled in sleep. On his left, the room slid sideways into darkness, where there existed, somewhere, a bed and, on it, a sleeping young woman. These items, though no doubt plain, pretentious or scuffed, were gilded to an inexpressible glamour by the drink and narcotics in Stephen's blood. Stephen remembers he was in evening dress – the real thing: a stiff collar that rubbed his neck, seamed trousers that flattered his long legs, a white waistcoat with, on it, a hash burn – but not why he was wearing this antiquarian costume. Also in the room, standing at one of the long windows and looking out towards Ireland, was Johnny Bellarmine, smoking; and between the windows, at a surface that might have been a desk or dressing-table, Vijay Subota was doing something Stephen did not want to look at.

The door pushed frictionally over the thick carpet. The dim passage-light brought in a stingy institutional note. Jane Bellarmine stood for a moment in the doorway, not quite upright; or rather, in Stephen's reconstructions at all those four o'clocks, her long dress hung in a strange way, as if her head were lolling on her shoulder or she leaned with one hand on the door-post; then she passed, stepped, ran over the carpet.

As she came by Stephen, without noting or seeing that admirably long, straight, clean, black-and-white and supine figure, she let out her breath; gasped; and vanished in the direction of the little table with its shaded lamp where Vijay Subota was at work.

It was this sense of her wanting, of a woman wanting something so badly she'd thrown all caution to the winds; of a stranger ministering to this want in the presence of her husband; of their common exhila-ration, suspended above town and beach – that disgusted Stephen beyond description; and, if he'd had a little insight into the world and his own nature, if his mind hadn't been so damn quick he'd actually thought about something for once in his life, he'd have seen that what frightened him had nothing to do with heroin and needles and a lot to do with female sexual affection. He didn't look round, though he sensed Vijay fiddling expertly with her taffeta sleeve, whimpering small comforts to her; and soon he couldn't look round, because Vijay filled his vision, had sat down on the sofa and put his hand on Stephen's hip, was saying something, narrative, tedious, evidently shocking.

Vijay Subota is dead: of an overdose some distance to the south and nearer sea-level than this hotel bedroom, and improbably, at least to Stephen, who never thought Vijay was in the business of dying or indeed of anything. Vijay's sad and picturesque career does not concern us, except to record the truth that a generation is winnowed, first grain by grain, and then in bushels. Vijay exists in these reconstructions in the hour before dawn, the hour known in his grandfather's village in Iran as the hour of the sheep and the wolf, when fear sprang at Stephen's throat for but one purpose. Vijay exists only to obscure Jane Bellarmine who is now seated, upright on a chair though lop-sided from her rolled-up sleeve, looking at her husband with a look I cannot describe, so helpless, hopeless is it. He looks at Ireland, smoking.

Between his dominant impulses, which were fear and possession, Stephen barely knew what to do with his bedside picture. He never thought to cash it in, though to what was then known as Fleet Street it had a money value: indeed, to certain newspapers, it was the nearest thing there was to money without having the Queen's head on it, a tungsten strip running down the middle and the signature of the chief cashier of the Bank of England. Like all assets, its money value rose and fell and rose again; reached a first zenith when Jane and Johnny Bellarmine enjoyed their social celebrity, subsided at their divorce and Jane's expatriation and was all but extinguished as the country lost interest in an intoxicated nobility; recovered, at Vijay's death, a modest scarcity value; and began to rise again, perpendicularly, with Jane's new fame as Jane Haddon, maiden champion of a ruined industry.

But Stephen was no blackmailer, and its value to him rose steadily every year, and always more than the inflation in memory, as we age, of our young happiness. Stephen prospered in the City, for the boom that followed the lowering of interest by the United States Federal Reserve in August 1982 was to his generation of financiers what a sanguinary war is to ambitious military officers; but in truth he had little interest in investment banking, none in being rich, and no City friends. He was alienated from his surviving family, not so much by bad blood as by his scholarships; and meanwhile his friends from school and university had fallen away, not into suicide or heroin or anything so lurid, but into time-swallowing jobs, suspicious wives or indifferent husbands, interesting children and a sort of armistice with the England of late century that Stephen vowed he would never sign. Stephen had just Jane, in person and in his imagination, and her ex-husband.

"It's not good for you, Jane! Can't you see? Celibacy is very, very dangerous. It'll send you mad. Impair your business judgement. Textiles is a public company. You have responsibilities to your share-holders, employees, suppliers, customers. I was talking to Alan Nixon just the other day, and he said, I'm a mite worried about Jane, she's a healthy young woman, she never seems to . . ."

"STOP IT!"

Jane had her eyes closed, her fists in her ears. Stephen felt like slinking away, through the swinging fire door, past the sexless sailing prints and the individual, picked-over dinner trays.

Jane pulled herself together and stood back from her door. "I'm sorry, Stephen. Come in. We'll have a drink and whatever. But you must leave me alone. Do you understand?"

"I understand, Jane."

Stephen woke with a sense of unbearable well-being. He felt swaddled in layers of security and delight. First, his hangover and whatever the residue of marijuana-intoxication is called; second, a ravenous hunger for fried food; then the anonymous hotel room and the windows whipped with rain and the wind that raced over the chimney pots and scuttled in the fire-place and whined in the Thermopane; and finally this forgotten town, the unfashionable county and the unfrequented sea, with just the sodium wire of last night's journey tying him to the world of anxiety. There was one item more, which composed and illuminated all the others, suspended the present, explained the past, disarmed the future. Sitting up, he saw the small depression in the white candlewick where she had lain, felt again the touch of her wool dress and, through it, her warm skin as they slept, back to back, affectionate, senseless and chaste.

Jane herself was in the dining room, reading the *Liverpool Post*, before a plate of cold toast and unopened mini-pots of jam.

He said: "You are just so incredibly stingy, Jane. You are the most highly remunerated woman in Britain and you're too fucking mean to stand yourself breakfast." Stephen caught the troubled waitress. "Could you please make that two Big Lancastrians? And the coffee extra-strong?"

Jane seemed absorbed in her newspaper. She said, without looking up: "Have you got to get down? I mean . . ."

Stephen made a telephoning gesture.

"You mean you haven't called Lizzie! For God's sake, Stephen, there's been incredible damage. A whole street washed into the sea at Hastings. Half London without power. Trees down all over the place. At least ten people killed. You have to do one thing or the other, Stephen. Can't you see?" Nine quid for bacon and eggs, it is a rip-off, too.

"Lizzie's at Petworth," he said, as if that were sufficient pardon.

"What about the Wall Street thing? I mean, don't you need to deal? I know they'll be working all weekend in New York. The paper only has the Dow at noon yesterday, but . . ."

"No. Shut up, Jane."

They borrowed wellington boots from the hotel and walked the length of the esplanade. At their left, waves soared and plunged at the sea-wall, engulfing them in salt and wet, so Stephen had to take off his glasses. Occasionally, they had to detour across great lakes of water that whipped up into peaks in the wind. The shops and arcades were shuttered. Blind without his glasses, Stephen felt happy as he had never been as an adult, embayed in the calm at the heart of some storm of money and history, the world's financial markets mysteriously frozen in their free fall, at the weekend. At the end of the esplanade, they climbed down some rotten concrete steps to a sodden beach and walked on. Jane bent against the wind in her coat, not talking. She was attempting to calculate, though Stephen did not know this, on the foundation of a single tentative estimate in the main story of the *Liverpool Post*, some large and complex arithmetic. Stephen, who never walked a mile without stopping to admire the view – a necessary progress in little England – was astonished by her persistence. Eventually, the beach gave way to fuming rocks, they climbed up to the sea wall, and Stephen found a bus-shelter and sat down; and because she continued to stand, finding and then lighting a cigarette, Stephen also stood up and made the short and interesting speech he had prepared on the walk. The reasons, he said, why they should marry were not simply that he loved and fancied her dreadfully, and had done so for years; or that he was faithful, as he had proved, and though fidelity isn't much, a sort of absence of anything worse, you can't do anything without it; or that they had much in common with each other and little with anybody else; or that Jane should have a baby fairly soon, and he'd be happy to assist in that enterprise; but that if they married they could keep something in the family, something valuable, which, if they moved apart or married elsewhere, would dissipate. In short, he said, as men do in certain Victorian novels, "May I hope, Jane? May I hope?"

"No," said Jane. "You may not." She turned to the sea and back again and said quickly: "I mean, what am I saying. Of course, you can hope. Who am I to say you cannot hope? Look, Stephen, we're talking past each other as the Germans say. Why do there have to be weddings and babies? Why do you make a narrative of your life that ends with weddings and babies? A house in Ladbroke Road? Timmy at Eton and Violet at St. Somebody's, Somewhere? Quarrels, reconciliations, grandchildren, illnesses, death or the dementias of old age? And all this resting, as it were, on some experience of unquestionable authority: for all I know, this conversation in a bus shelter in a storm in a town whose name I don't know but is up the coast from Southport, Lancashire.

"I don't believe in these things. I believe that England is disintegrating and that quite soon no family will know the name of its grandparents. You know, when I was married to Johnny, I never thought that he belonged to me; or that house or all that fortune in things and money. It belonged to somebody else, not me, to *Country*

Life or Mrs Moran or all those snobs in bright corduroys who came before lunch or we went to them before lunch. They looked at me as if I were a piece of history, the seventh countess who is between the sixth countess and the eighth countess, in a line stretching back and forth out of sight like the Scottish kings that appear to Macbeth in the Fourth Act. It didn't seem to occur to these people that there might be no eighth countess – oh all right, that's Candida – but I mean no ninth or tenth; and no Wexley Park and no Johnny by Batoni in its golden frame; and that they themselves were the last gasp of history.

"History, I now see, is tragic, but not in the way we all think. Not because of war and murder and famine and depression. The tragedy of history lies in that nobody understands the tiniest part of it as it is happening. We live through it without understanding a bloody thing.

"Look, Stephen, I live in the past like you, but I do not, like you, treat it as a guide to the present or a promise of the future. I have felt some love and affection in my life, which seem to me to have been authentic, but they are like the coin that Nikolai finds in his waistcoat pocket outside the station in Roulettenburg: a promise of unimaginable wealth, but only if a series of favourable accidents occurs, again and again and again without fail, which – and we should never have got into nineteenth-century novels – is improbable, to say the least, with two zeroes on the wheel. This wealth is not, as it is to you, inevitable to me, but rather extremely unlikely, and so you keep the coin but also the dream of possibility."

"Not every bloke's like Johnny, you know."

"Evidently." Jane waved her cigaretted hand. She still spoke at break-neck pace, but the interruption had ruined her temper. "What's the matter with you, Stephen? Why do you live in this fraudulent old English past? You're Jewish, for God's sake. Your father was a grocer . . ."

"Pharmacist, actually, Jane."

"It must have been that bloody school."

Jane, like almost all women who have ever given thought to the matter, disapproved of Eton and its passionate, lifelong friendships and its catapult into the top storey; and also the conviction in its pupils that all problems were social in aspect, might be solved by a call or visit or introduction. Stephen had been first scholar in the Election, seven places ahead of Johnny, and there was not a day when these two facts did not return to please or console him.

He said: "I live in the past, Jane, because that's where I was happy, with you, and Johnny."

"You were young. Most people enjoy being young. And now you're older, not just in years, but because the world has turned, and nobody cares about a lot of ex-druggies, snobs, sentimentalists, frauds. We thought we'd demolished the world, but in reality we'd only picked at the wallpaper! All we did was make love, as if we'd invented it! But now . . . but now. Look at it out there!" She glanced round to find something to embody her idea, and saw rain and heaving sea, which were not the thing at all. "Look at me, trying to save a broken-down old plant which is uncompetitive even at £4.50 an hour while the Lon Nok plant in Sichuan pays girls of fourteen twenty-five cents. All I can do is delay the thing, make an orderly withdrawal, let them down lightly, because one day Alan is going to get on an aeroplane to China and then that's the end of us. And why am I doing it? Because my mother worked there or rather, not even that, but because nobody else wants to do it; because I've fallen out of the world of TV and mobile phones and protected sex, and burrowed into my little corner, just as you have and Johnny. We're too few and inbred to have any evolutionary future. We're like lemurs or the Men of the Forties in Turgenev. To the people of the Eighties we are a joke."

"It doesn't matter, Jane. All that matters is that I love you. That's beyond fashion or history. It's a piece of eternity. I will love you and you can fuck off."

Jane thought: If you had some knowledge of yourself, some tiny scrap of insight, you'd see that dating Johnny Bellarmine's cousin and trying to marry his ex-wife were not accidental events but linked by a connection that would be obvious to a sick child. But though Stephen took a lot of lip from Jane, she saw that to have suggested, at the moment of his solemn proposal of marriage, that he was gay, was going somewhat too far. It was also unfair, for she suspected Stephen's need to inhabit his friends' existences, and so comprehensively that his company became intolerable, arose in a discontent not at his sex but his biography: and that the three of them – Johnny, Lizzie, Jane – had somehow replaced his lost familiar paradise. Jane collected herself.

"I'm sorry, Stephen. And you are right to say I would have trouble replacing you as a friend. Now, let's go back and gorge ourselves on scampi and Vouvray."

On the walk back, they were merry, though the wind was up again and the sea was a plunging, turbulent green. The heart is a resilient muscle and Stephen chose to ignore all that Jane had said, except her last two sentences. And Jane herself, I'm sure, was too modest and intelligent to exclude a future with Stephen, for who can know the mind of God? Climbing up to their rooms, going past him as he shouldered open the fire door for her, over the roar of the wind and the clatter of the kitchen, she pointed her finger at his chest and said: No. By which negative, she confirmed the subsistence of a positive, which sent Stephen skipping over the flowered corridor carpet to his bedroom and into deep sleep. He thought he had advanced his emotional project by many, many squares. He never saw Jane walking up and down her room in a bath-towel, her arms crossed beneath her bust, or smoking, too tired and sad to enter her cold candlewick bed.

5

1980. Somewhere in England. Whizzing through mown country. Miles of fields and hedges, I didn't know there was so much of England that wasn't town; or that it never gets dark. Dizzy with drink and heroin. Also not having a driving licence. Crying, though that may be just chaff through the open windows; and happy, so happy, because I never did love Johnny and he didn't love me but I love his car which goes straight like an arrow to wherever I point it and the hissing wind and his hand in my pants and the way his head is upright in his lapels and the bottle he holds for me which says – I'm noticing these things – Château Beychevelle 1959; and because I've told him I'm going away, I think tomorrow, to fulfil my destiny (which includes my class destiny as the bastard and orphaned trash of unrentable industrial processes) and this is a spell at Harvard Business School and then to work until I drop; while Johnny will fulfil his, which is, after a decent interval spent in some nice place like Resolute Bay, North-West Territories, marriage to a girl whose singular or only virtue is that she is nothing that I am, an estate in northern England, farms, most of Auckland, New Zealand, a very good racemare called, ironical-anachronistical, Plain Jane, commissions on this and that, the House of Peers and, pray God, a bewildered and reactionary old age and the far-off sound of children squabbling on the gravel, oh my darling.

When Johnny and I meet, which is not often, we cross rooms; but we do not touch. I come away from these meetings, which are at second weddings or events to do with TV, not with regret for an abbreviated love affair – or even the consolation of doomed love that spares the lovers tedium and mortality – but in shock: that the two of us, so lucky in our ways, could do nothing for our country or our age but smash each other to smithereens. Even in public, Johnny's frame reverberates so I reach out with my fingers, as if to deaden a ringing glass, then fumble with cigarettes. I want to speak, but I have no voice, as in a nightmare. Candida sees me, and comes up; and we talk for a bit, friendly-like; and then they go away.

I want to say: What business had you with me, you and your mother? Stuck-up, invulnerable, pig-headed, kind, you wouldn't listen, would you? Is it my fault you wouldn't listen, that time you walked towards me across a city garden and I said, I'll wound you, my honey, you won't make your three score years and ten, I'll take your life and make it just like mine? You have nobody but yourself to blame.

It was evening. There were roses that burned in the half-light. His eyes, too, seemed to give back the day's stored sunshine: as if he had spent the day in fields or walking on dusty highways. His jacket, which was of blue velvet, was gashed at the left shoulder and I thought, Needs a girl's fingers, does it, my bonny? I wanted time to stop; and Dr Wright, the boy called Stephen, all those awful girls, to become motionless as trees or street-lamps; and I to run through the house and run and run and never stop running. His eyes glittered with laughter, not at the poor girl trembling by the roses, hand to mouth, the other across her breast, but at the sheer luck of the thing: as if to say, What a small world, that you and I have met in it, Miss I'm-afraid-I-don't-know-your-name!

In his car, which was a Mini, we stared for some time at the trees and miserable houses and the driving-lesson street. I didn't want him to look at me, and he didn't. Then he said, very slowly and staring straight ahead, "So you don't want to go to Cercio's with the others; and you don't want to go back to your college." He glanced at me and back to the street, still smiling, and said, "Jane, I've had a brilliant idea." Then he started the car.

I wish I'd never seen beauty. Everything about him was beautiful, and I'd never seen anything beautiful, so that if today, walking along a beach in Lancashire, I see a tumbling sea green as soapstone, I turn away from the association of beauty lest it tear the stitches in my heart. I wish I'd never known happiness or sat waiting in his room with its silly rafters and incessant views of spires and fields, while girls drank Coke and moaned and Stephen stole glances at me from over his reefers. I'd lost my underwear and didn't know where to go to wash. I sat on the windowsill, petrified and ashamed, till the staircase clattered, the room quickened, cries of Johnny! Darling! Man! And your eye flickered round the imbecile room, you raised both hands, you said: Guys, I've got to do it, now! Please! Yes! Great! Eight! Sure! Cercio's! And as they gathered up their things and moaned and traipsed, you grumbled, offhand-like, Jane, did you by any chance . . . ? So I turned, there by the sitting-room door, and saw you at the other door, bowing a little, like an ambassador, and as I stepped towards you, I felt like the Empress of all the Russias.

The day I met his mother, she gave me a jewel. She taught me French and double-entry accounting. Each morning at ten, I sat on a stool with a blue cushion with a crown while she gabbled at me or dictated letters to her secretary. I learned from her that loving was not some sickness, for how can it be, if you can do it twice and even in the same family, and I imagine, though I haven't tried this and don't think I shall, more often or even as often as you like. But because all the love I ever felt was for his family, I dream of fells and icebergs, and these are my reality from which I fall into a doze of tube trains and newspaper interviews and Alan Nixon on the phone. And they were there, every morning as I came down, Johnny at Hawaii, Johnny in the Bering Sea, there, as you poured coffee from the breakfast flask; and Meg, so pretty and gay in her cow-girl's cap above the satsumas you'd think God must draw her to his bosom, which he did, in child-bed, the bastard, and Johnny went a-sailing, and lay with maid no more, no more, and lay with maid no more. (And I have seen our Fair Friends laugh and jeer at the Captain from the shore, calling him Old, and Good for nothing.) For this family, the past was not extinguished but was, on the contrary, inextinguishable. I never met a family that so fed on time. And oh, the hours of these people, the days that never ended and the early nights, you'd think that the whole world could be happy like this, if it let the clocks run on and on, and chime, as you opened a door or ran for the post, four for the quarter, eight for the half and Lord knows how many for the hour and the next just as sweet-smelling. Oh Johnny, why did you invite me into your house?

That August, his mother fell in the library. She lay in an avalanche of books. Johnny had to pull the books off her, one by one, as if they'd been screes. I was left alone in a ticking house and windy garden. I could hear the devils bickering in the rick-yard. At night, they swooped and leered at me from the bed-posts. In her will, she left me a tenanted farm, the only copy of John Law's *Reckoning of the Chances at Hazzard, Basset, Faro etc.*, two million pounds in money after duty and the *vanitas* picture by Gysbrechts from her sitting room, with a skull, and a glass half-filled with wine, and a dead heron, and a twist of tangerine peel. I tried to give these things back, but Johnny wouldn't take them, and so I married him. I must emphasise that taking heroin was all my idea: I needed a friend, a third person, for I was lonely after his mother's death. Johnny never took intoxicants. Once he asked me not to, but then he never said anything more than once.

You see, I thought that matter was indifferent to me. I thought that the stone and silk and glass would survive me; that the hills were your furniture and the moors your carpets and the tarns would not hold my reflection. I didn't know that they existed only by your will, which I extinguished, as a smoker shakes out a match. Oh Johnny, I wish I'd never lived.

They say the heart is a resilient muscle. Bouncing on to the Triboro Bridge, I saw a heavenly city and said: "Who put that there?" I thought I hadn't said it out loud but, in the partition, the driver's face was brilliant with teeth. We stopped on a street called Lenox Avenue, so he could shout at some men lolling on chairs, and as they cursed and laughed and slapped their knees, I got out and walked into a tenement that said Negro Christian Girls Association (1923) and lay down on a bed. The super brought me bottles of a liquor called Mount Gay, and sometimes I woke to see him leaning against the doorpost. Ambulances invaded my sleep, and sweat and blows and cries of agony and pleasure. Later, I went to a Lebanese doctor on West 110th Street, who did acupuncture on the side. Afterwards, I used to stop at Gray's Papaya where Broadway crosses Amsterdam Avenue, because Donna at the Negro said the hot dogs were the best in the city. Once I stood on the street corner, in drifts of paper napkins and soft-drink cups, while sensations barrelled through me like yellow cabs: the fizz of Dr Hobeika's electric needles, the tumult of salt and fat and beef in my mouth, and diagonally across them, retreating into the distance, gaping and sad and long and old as Broadway itself, my lost marriage. That day I discovered white New York. I rode down to his lawyer on Wall Street and Mr Rothenstein came out of his office in his braces, just to look at me. I had to divorce him, you see, so he could live.

I did a semester at Cambridge. The work was elementary. I dreamed of meeting the author of *The Imaginary Iceberg*, conducted conversations with her as we walked, clinking, across Harvard Yard or sat dazed over coffee in the Coop. I enrolled in her class, which was at MIT. The verses glutted my imagination:

> We'd rather have the iceberg than the ship,
> although it meant the end of travel.

Arriving for class, I saw over shoulders a typewritten notice:

MISS BISHOP IS IN THE HOSPITAL
& IS VERY SORRY SHE WILL BE UNABLE
TO MEET HER CLASSES THIS WEEK

I felt giddy at my compounding losses, like a gambler. So I left and did an internship at Handel & Wind on Water Street. Some mornings, I was blinded by a copper sun as my cab skimmed towards the East River tunnel and La Guardia, or I stood in wonder, on Park Avenue in February, while clouds engulfed the colossal buildings which seemed to be the trunks of ancient technical trees with their heads lost in heaven. On 11th Street and Fifth Avenue, I saw a little brownstone house with a stoop and a basement, a door and one window, and two more in the mansard; and I wished – for the only time in my life – that

I still had a little of the money your mum gave me. For in the loveliest and kindest of all the cities of the earth, I was mended, as it were.

And you, my darling, have you your own America or is every place to you a place of diminished interest and amenity, as to a fallen angel? There's not a day when I don't think of your ancestor, who just sailed away: trusting in God, and his Newcastle ships, and his men from the dales and his Birmingham compass; on and on and on, though the timbers burst, and the men rave at the bare-breasted girls on the shore, and your eyes splinter with novelty and terror; and one by one the sailors fall asleep at their stations and are lowered into the sea, and each new landing is a bloody battle over a longboat or iron nails. I think if you could see him, if he were there one evening, at his desk from the *Good Hope*, working late on his despatch – for sailors, they say, are hard to count among the living or the dead – and she's gone to bed, and you come in for one last cigarette in front of the fire, and your eyes cross, just for an instant of an instant, you'd know and the weight would fall from me and I could get through all this.

6

The political committee of the Workers Party, the highest authority below the Central Committee, held its weekly meeting at ten o'clock on a Monday morning at the converted garage off Streatham High Street that had been the party's headquarters since 1959. Outside the street had changed, print frocks given way to jeans and then shell-suits, jewellers had become wine bars and then video stores, but the Workers Party, which reckoned history in the long dialectic of human consciousness and misery, took no notice.

The men and women entering the room, the men in shop assistants' suits from thirty years before – fifty-shilling suits, as it were, as if the shilling hadn't disappeared in 1971 or the chain that made them eight years later, its freeholds bought for nothing by a fashion retailer tilting at Reuben & Style – while the women carried in their hair styles or their trousers or even the way they walked the faint exhilaration of their break-out in the 1960s. For revolution is a damn long, hard grind, and it will take a life and crumple it as if it were paper, and throw it away. It is not for the young or professors or dandies or lovers, nor for the merely gifted, here on this Monday morning, 19 October, 1987, off Streatham High Street.

Last to enter, but not by tradition – which was small-bourgeois and anyway a present to the watchers of the Security Service – was Sean McVie, the general secretary of the Workers Party. Bustling in, head bent, swinging a briefcase, he gave the impression of tireless and efficient hurry, as if he had come straight from a meeting – Glasgow, Wigan, Merthyr, Portsmouth – and would rush on from this meeting, losing himself in the corner of the InterCity or reading in the passenger seat of a car filling up at a lit service station. McVie was old, though how old nobody knew. Legends encrusted his antique suit like medals on a veteran. Had he not, as correspondent of the *Daily Worker*, reported witheringly on the Moscow Trials, corrected the proofs of the Transitional Programme in Principe, closed the old man's unaffrighted eyes in Coyoacan?

I do not know his documentary, as opposed to historical materialist biography, and I don't think anybody can know; though I have seen his file with the Security Service, itself largely drawn from the archive of the Communist Party of Great Britain in Hackney Wick. He was born in Scotland, probably in Fife, in the years of the Great War, the son perhaps of a minister of the Kirk, and made his living at first as a huckster. He emerges out of this mist of Scotland and folklore in 1938, when he attempted to break up a CP rally in Dumfries. In the archive biography, which is dated 1948, he is described as "a good demagogic speaker, with a good library at his disposal", who had married one Betty *née* Russell (Wandsworth branch, exp. 1938) but since divorced; had worked at Amalgamated Engineering in Preston during the Second World War, organising strikes against the express order of the Comintern and the line of the CPGB; and his politics, well, they were ultra-left.

At the end of the war, when the revolution predicted in the Transitional Programme obstinately stayed away, he entered the Labour Party as leader of a clandestine group known eventually to Transport House as The Group; but recruitment was slow; and the enterprise was saved from extinction only by the events of 1956 in Moscow and Budapest and, when it was again becalmed ten years later, by those of 1968 in Paris and Peking. The party was founded at the Hammersmith Odeon in 1970 and by 1974, the Workers Party – the only party that could lead the working class of Britain to power in an insurrectionary general strike – could muster ten thousand members. Numbers had by the time of our story dwindled to twelve hundred, one quarter of those in arrears on their membership. A damn, long, hard grind.

As the comrades took their seats, complained about the coffee, put out their cigarettes if they had them – for smoking was proletarian but also undisciplined – McVie glanced at his papers and then plunged into the world of war, revolutions and chaos and the death-agonies of late capitalism. And if any of these men and women – Tom Sale of Newcastle Poly, Fifty-Sixer, ideologue, or Sheila Wright, once the mini-skirted firebrand of the Young Socs. (before their expulsion from the Labour Party), or Bill Tuohy, the Kiwi editor of *Workers Week*, hard-bitten, also an MI5 agent though he sometimes forgot it – if any of them ever felt that time moved in the shorter rhythms of TV and skirt hems and orgasms, McVie soon put him right. And her.

"Motherwell," he said.

The political committee was not a place for Sunday rhetoric; but the history in which Sean McVie lived, the tumult at the Grand Palais, the barricades on Usbetskaya Street, the bodies in the Landwehr Canal, were like distant mountains in a snapshot. Britain had had its Thermidor, when the Thatcher-Carrington axis, uniting the vengeful small shopkeepers with a decayed aristocracy, smashed the working class in 1984 and won the middle class to Bonapartism. What remained were the evolving consequences of these occurrences, and their dialectical resolution. Oh, that bright morning, how history surged down Streatham High Street like a wave!

"Motherwell. The crisis of monopoly capitalism on the one hand, and the emergence of primitive state capitalism in the traditional lands of colonial oppression on the other, combined with a shrinking world market, has led to the expected attack on wages in Britain as a preparation for the final pauperisation of the British working class. There will be a strike at the Associated British Textiles plant in Motherwell, which will not be successful in its aims. The question facing the Workers Party at this historical conjuncture is whether it should lead or otherwise seek to direct this doomed enterprise."

It was a curiosity of the Workers Party, that members spoke strictly by seniority; and women, ideally, not at all: a peculiarity shared, by coincidences not of my making, with the Jockey Club (Chief Steward: The Earl of Bellarmine) and the Council of Lloyd's, on which

R.W. Turpe served with such distinction at this period. Bill Tuohy said: "We have an asset at the plant."

This intelligence fell like a stone into the gathering: not because of the Security Service slang – for the Workers Party resembled its shadow in more ways than I can describe – but because it was many years since the party had had any representation in manufacturing industry; since, to be precise, the autumn of 1974 when a hundred-strong group at Austin at Longbridge had been expelled over a dispute as to whether the situation was a revolutionary one or merely pre-revolutionary.

I am not sure whether, in speaking, Bill Tuohy had in mind the prosperity of the Workers Party or of Mrs Rimington behind her blast curtains in Curzon Street, and I doubt if he knew himself. He could no longer distinguish his lives, for they all got him down. "There's a girl named Cathy McKay, works as a machinist at the plant, talked to Deb Gully at the gate and is now at the White House with her. Says she's a sister of the woman who runs ABT . . ."

"That's Lady Bellarmine, as was."

Sheila Wright was astonished, not for the first time, at McVie's uncanny knowledge of the fine social grain of the British high bourgeoisie: a knowledge scarcely to be justified in that these people were mere character masks for the control of the means of production. The thought awoke an old suspicion, which was just as soon allayed: for had not she herself, with the cadres, hiked up from the White House (as the party's College of Marxist Education was known to all but McVie) to gape down at Wexley Park and its now-ruined beech woods and gloat over the destiny of the house of Bellarmine?

"I fail to see," said Tom Sale, "the significance of this blood relation."

"Well, if you don't see it," said McVie, "I don't imagine it need be explained."

Sale flushed, not with anger – for he was terrorised beyond anger – but in shame. McVie continued: "What is required is the most scrupulous analysis of conditions at the plant, and an interview with the young woman in question. I believe it would be the sense of this committee that Comrade Wright should travel up to the college after the day's work and question the woman."

There was no vote. Votes were rare at the Workers Party after '56.

The meeting handled other business of small interest to us and history; for the great event of that day, the fall in the Dow Jones Industrial Average of five hundred points had yet to occur, and anyway capitalism is exceptionally prone to crisis, as everybody knows. Sheila returned to her tasks and to her pride and joy, a cloned IBM PC; but a sort of dread ate at her all day, made her gulp her sandwich at lunch and spill her tea. Sheila had given her life to the Workers Party, also her beauty and the possibility of motherhood: first, as leader of the YouSos and then, for nineteen years, as McVie's personal secretary and friend. She had lived all the party's triumphs and setbacks, the Ally Pally rally of '74, the meeting with Gaddafi at Sirte, the police raid on the White House, the split over *perestroika* in '85, and this dread was something never far from her, was the companion of her life. As she was locking up at five, the telephone rang and she realised, for the first time, the locus of her dread.

"Sheila," said McVie from his flat round the corner in Tadema Road. He used her first name in private. "I believe it would be helpful if I accompanied you to the college this evening. I have some questions I would like to pose myself."

Sheila Wright put down the telephone and, to her overwhelming relief, burst into tears.

Meanwhile two miles to the north, Jane, as can readily be imagined, was conspiring with high officials of government against the class which had brought her to birth.

Thomas Waldo Burke, the minister of state at the Department of Trade and Industry, was handsome, clever, and rich beyond computation; but each night, in his flat in Marsham Street or at his Lutyens house in Sussex, he dreamed convulsively of the highest office. His dreams were of newspaper copy, articles both leaden and frivolous, remote and familiar; where, buried in the tailings of some exhausted speculation, behind a parade of R & S ties and a patter of brown shoes, there'd be . . . and Tom Burke to Paymaster General and a seat in Cabinet; or . . . the seat in Cabinet that Mr Tom Burke so obviously deserves.

By day, he intrigued against the Secretary of State, wrote papers to the Prime Minister that he delivered himself to the stony policemen at Downing Street and, each weekend, invited reporters to his home, collected them from distant railway stations, watched them guzzle his Yquem and mangle his cigars and ignore his lovely wife, for had not Bhose in the *Mail* written just last week . . . and old Tom Burke to Transport? Not that Transport was particularly glorious, but it was a seat in Cabinet, even down table, and in the presence of his leader whom he loved not because she embodied the puerile chauvinism he'd held intact since Eton, but as a man loves a woman. Also he'd ban caravans by day and all post-1957 Jaguars.

The problem, as Tom saw clearly, was that he was lazy beyond description; also rude, ruder than the dandies that used to stand in the big bay window of White's in the time of Brummell; and so scared of being old and dying, every girl tore at his heart and, for a moment, if she smiled at him, took away his fear: in short, that it was only through the despotism the British submit to from an able prime minister that he held on even to his modest position. For she, though Tom never suspected it, loved him in her way.

"Jane," he shouted, standing up and coming round his desk. He stared into her eyes, while a civil servant looked down impatiently at the dark river. "Johnny was mad to let you go. Barking mad."

"You asked to see me. I imagine it's about the Motherwell site."

"We're rather . . ." said the civil servant.

"Look, Jane. I don't give a toss if you close it down, serve all those idlers and Trots right. Look, sit down, will you? Did they give you tea or whisky and all?"

Jane sat down and waited while Tom strode up and down on his Huntsman legs and black Lobb feet.

"We have a political problem, Jane. Now that shit McCabe at British Steel has closed Ravenscraig, unemployment on Clydeside is . . ."

He cupped his hand to his ear. The official, fiddling with his folder but not opening it, said:

"Twenty-one per cent. Thirty-three per cent for males . . ."

"I don't employ men at the site . . ."

". . . and so on, little chiseller. The fact is, Jane, the political fact is that this party, this glorious party, this party so rich in tradition, has precisely three MPs north of the border and will have two when Tam Menteith goes to his long home, which can't be soon enough for me . . ."

"The minister also means that there are powerful economic arguments. It is a structurally weak region, within the definition . . ."

"Shut up, you! Mrs Haddon is trying to talk!"

Tom caught his breath.

"Look, Jane, beautiful Jane, if it were left to me, I'd say: Close the fucker. Now. But a certain lady . . ." He tailed off. His face took on a look of comical melancholy.

Jane waited an age and then said: "Management's proposal for capital investment financed through a partial deferment of wages was rejected by all the plant's unions at members' meetings this morning."

"What about ACAS or whatever those pinko dons are called?"

"We are automatically in ACAS. Excuse me, minister, but I am not free. The plant is losing money. I depend for seventy per cent of my sales on a single customer, who is no longer prepared to take product from Motherwell . . ."

"You mean that common little git, Nixon? We'll put him on a commission to streamline Whitehall!"

"I do not own Associated British Textiles, minister. I am answerable to a number of constituencies, including the other plant workforces, the board and the company's shareholders."

"Cunt off, Jane! Don't come that crap with shareholders. You mean a lot of overpaid little twerps in the City like Lamont before he got lucky."

"I believe Mrs Haddon meant . . ."

"Fuck off, you! Just fuck off! I'm talking to fucking Jane."

He put a hand on her shoulder and, with the gentlest pressure, directed her to the door. In the outer office, where the secretaries tapped away, he said: "Jane, you have to have dinner with me. We'll go to Milton's. I fancy you, Jane. You're making me ill. You're just . . . you're just . . . you're just so bonny."

"I don't think that would be a good idea, minister. You'll only feel worse afterwards."

"Even my secretaries won't sleep with me."

Tom walked her to the obsolescent lifts. "Please, Jane," he said, running his hand through his long hair, which was still thick and black. "You do what you think best and I'll try and get these prats to support you. You know more about this in your little finger than we do in the whole fucking department." Suddenly, he glared at her. A thought had come on him and, as with everything to do with Tom Burke, like an explosion. "You're not doing this just to show you've got balls, are you, because if you are, I'll . . ."

"No. And I haven't."

"Yes. Good. Very good," he said vaguely. Then: "Well, try not to have a strike, if you can conceivably avoid it."

The lift arrived, expiring. He put out his hand:

"*Der Johnny macht mir Sorgen.*" He said this sentence, I'm anxious about Johnny, in German, not simply because he had a house at Partenkirchen and loved the language, but also because of his intense admiration for Hitler as a military leader, in which opinion at that time, he was, I believe, in a minority of one. He regained his poise and said: "What's the matter with bloody Wall Street?"

He strode back towards the wriggling secretaries.

The doors closed on Jane. She would have liked to have had dinner at Milton's, and even to have slept with Tom Burke, who seemed a very nice man; but she knew she had to be in the office all evening, because of the time difference with New York.

Her direct line was flashing self-importantly. She picked it up and heard, as she always did, just for an instant, the tumbling Atlantic.

"Jane." The voice was America-French. "It's Charles Lauriston."

"Sir Charles! How nice to hear from you."

"Do you know what that half-witted chairman of yours has just done? He shot the Quotron! He shot the Quotron!" The words sounded delicious in his hotelier's voice. "He has ten millions in put options, and can't collect, ha ha! He can't get anybody to take the other side of the trade."

Down the line, there was a shout and a lady's shriek. Sir Charles Lauriston's voice deepened. "What we're witnessing here, Jane, is a systemic failure. Systemic failure. I warned John Phelan at the New York Stock Exchange. I warned Nick Brady at Treasury. I warned Alan Greenspan at the Fed. That we would be confronted . . ."

"Jane! Jane!" Lord Doncaster's voice came on the line.

"Hello, Chairman. I hear you've been taking out your frustrations . . ."

"I've looked into the heart of darkness, Jane. There was this line of IBM, crossed at sixteen, six-bloody-teen, when the thing opened at a hundred and fifty . . ."

"Can't you go down yourself to the floor to trade?"

"You must be fucking mad, Jane. People are dying in there. Mid-town's totally gridlocked."

"There's the subway."

Lord Doncaster did not ride the New York City subway. He said: "I love you, Jane."

There was a roar like thunder. Ah, thought Jane, a joke. They're playing a joke on me.

Screams and laughter, diminishing. Jane tried to imagine the scene: the suite littered with people and luxury items and, all over them, a boredom so black and acrid she felt her stomach turn. Sir Charles Lauriston came back on:

"I just wanted to say what a fine job I think you're doing, Jane. The orderly retrenchment of an uncompetitive industry. And if you have any trouble with that chippy little turd Alan Nixon, just call me, will you? Tell him I told you so. I'll buy his bloody company . . ."

Jane flipped over the back page of the *Financial Times*, and found Stores, General. She said: "Reuben & Style has, I believe, Sir Charles, a market capitalisation of eleven thousand eight hundred and thirty-one million pounds and the most highly regarded management in Britain . . ."

"It's financeable," he said. "Martin could do it in a morning." He lost interest. "It's a matter of competition not subsidisation," and so on into a rigmarole that Sir Charles Lauriston unfurled with unfailing regularity, ever since he had quit England for ever in 1978 (except for visits to Epsom and a household he maintained in Chelsea Square). Then he said: "The deflationary fat is in the fire, Jane."

"Yes," she said. "Thank you for calling me, Sir Charles."

She stayed at Burlington Street till the New York and Chicago markets closed, drinking the rum Pete kept for her in his desk. At some point, she thought: My townsman, the moral philosopher and political economist Adam Smith, tells us that the pursuit of money is instinctive, rational, beneficial to society and sufficient explanation of human history. Isn't it time somebody examined these rash assertions?

It is a mile from Hawksmoor's masterpiece to the road that follows the park wall towards the village of Wexleydale, so Johnny, as he drew shut the curtains of his bedroom, could never have seen the white Vauxhall containing Sheila Wright and Sean McVie, though it passed his park gates at that instant and the inside light was on, because McVie was reading.

Johnny said to his wife, pale before her dinner tray. "Five hundred points on the index. Pandemonium. Like 1929 but quite a bit worse."

"What does it mean for our stock exchange?" Candida had just invested three thousand pounds in a unit trust selected for her by Mrs Turpe, and this money meant more to her than all her married millions.

"Down and down and then, I suspect, up again. Unless the whole system is bust, and it doesn't have the feel of that."

"Are we finished?" Candida remembered to say.

"Not, it appears," said Johnny and came over and sat on a chair he pulled up to the bed. "Are those things working?"

"Not really."

He put his hand on her forehead.

"Why won't you talk to Uncle Roddie? You never listen to my family."

"I do."

7

If Johnny Bellarmine had an idea of beauty, it was of cool horses under green trees. He had seen them in 1981, at Newmarket races, at a blistering July Meeting. He'd been interested by a small wood of old beeches behind the paddock and, walking into it in his grey suit and trilby, seen men in bright silks and horses in harness stepping in and out of dappled shade.

It was only later that year, when the walls of his study at Wexley Park fluttered with computer print-outs, that he realised that it was the mathematics that interested him. He ignored the fashionable blood, the Northern Dancers and Nearcos and Ribots, not because he could not afford it, but because its virtue was all too evident: what he sought, in the antique crossings and nicks of blood and progeny, was something miraculous; and in this, too, he sought appeal against his fate. He settled in the end for a Hungarian stallion, who had never won a race, but who, at his eighth grandsire on the distaff side, had a blank: an animal not recorded in the stud-books of Hungary, Germany, England, Ireland, France, Italy, Russia or the United States. The horse stood, if that is the word, in County Kerry, and the nomination fee was forty pounds Irish. The result, a bay filly foaled late in 1983, he named Plain Jane: a name which was later considered awfully clever, since she was by Ugly Duckling out of Mirror Girl.

Plain Jane, who really was quite plain, a poor walker, with a blaze and three white socks, and very lazy, developed slowly even for a late foal and did not race at two. At three, the training stable at Malton in

Yorkshire was disabled with equine herpes. She won both her starts at four. The second of these, a race at Ascot in Berkshire in July called the King George and Queen Elizabeth Stakes, she won by eighteen lengths, defeating the Derby winners of England, France, Ireland and Italy and the winner of the previous year's English and Irish Oaks. They came in like washing in a high wind. Piggott, as he dismounted and lifted her saddle, said through his cleft palate, "Hard held, Johnny," and then, as if regretting his garrulousness, "Useful sort." Johnny kissed the mare on her soft nose and sensed her unused speed and willingness, and her inexhaustible stamina. He said, "That's more than enough, my darling."

Back in the box, Johnny was looking out through glass over the emptying racecourse, the blown litter and roaring drunks, when the Duke of Norfolk came in in a morning-coat with a caterers' employee, both very angry, carrying four bottles of bad champagne; and the message, delivered through a closed mouth, Her Majesty would be happy for you to drink your champion's health. Johnny thought: She's jealous of me, of all people: the most miserable of all her subjects, silly old bird. Still Candida, falling in a curtsey like an upset house of cards as the Queen came in to taste her wine, was pleased.

What he didn't expect was that, two months later, he would be offered the Jockey Club, which in those days meant the management of the English and Scottish racing business, that sustained a betting turnover of four thousand million pounds a year. It was a pastime in, as it were, galloping decline, in that the English public had discovered there were other recreations, less uncomfortable, expensive and raffish, and less brutally segregated according to social class: notably television. Johnny sensed that, even in his extreme self-mortification – the divorce became absolute that October– this was going it a bit, but he accepted. He knew he was not popular: that those men in Newmarket, pickled in the past and money, drink, horses and girls, needed somebody from the nobility who was also intelligent and conscientious, which reduced the field to almost nothing; that this person had to be somehow remote from society, so that when he failed, it would have no social consequence; that they hated him for retiring the mare, keeping her in the lap of luxury at Wexley, not even breeding from her but letting her consort promiscuously with intact horses of every description, a foal in her belly, schoolchildren on her back, wet-eyed Irishmen in raincoats gazing at her from the rails while their minicabs turned in the park gates; and that he hadn't been very nice to his beautiful first wife. This last objection almost prevented his appointment: though how that was material to his ability to manage an industry in severe crisis quite beats me, and anyway the men were too lazy or simple or plastered to investigate further.

In this, his first paying job at the age of twenty-nine, Johnny felt haunted by Jane. Johnny did not believe, as I do, that the deployment of females might revive a moribund British commerce, for he did not think in assertions; but he knew that the business intelligence in his family had been its women: his mother, Johnny the navigator's mother, and, briefly, the young woman known as Pretty Meg. It had been her mother-in-law's practice to divert the fabulous cash flow from the coal mines on the estate – twenty thousand pounds a year in 1755 – into mortgages on the estates of improvident neighbours either in Northumberland or the West Indies and into the primitive government securities known as Consols or Consolidated Annuities; but, as the estate books showed in beautiful copperplate and lucid Italian accounting, the year of her son's marriage brought a shift in investment: towards such risky enterprises as the financing of coal shipments to Southwark and Antwerp, and the purchase of return cargoes; shipbuilding in the yard that was later to make the *Good Hope* and *Paraclete*; and house-building in Newcastle and Bloomsbury; and this style of business persisted, even after Meg had died and old Lady Bellarmine picked up the reins again during her son's travels. I imagine the *rentier* existence does not appeal to cowmaids. (No doubt, had Meg lived, she would have founded a bank, fenced the park with spouting chimneys and made of Newcastle the second city of empire. Or maybe not. Death occurs at the moment the imagination fails.)

In 1985, there were sixty-seven racecourses in England and Scotland, of which Johnny thought fifty were redundant. He knew that Jane would have sold them to developers, and used the proceeds to finance improvements in comfort for the public, an increase in prize money and a breeder's premium, which would have kept the best blood-stock in England and also repatriated it from the United States and the Far East. He rejected this course of action, not just because he associated it with Jane, but because he was a softie: he could not bear that these race-tracks, many of them in the middles of towns or just on their edges, not be preserved as an amenity for the public. He demanded, with a minimum of tact and no warning, that the large off-course betting companies sequester a portion of the turnover from bets placed in bookies' offices – first five per cent, and then four – and this be handed over to the Jockey Club for investment in the racecourse facilities, additional prize money and the premium.

Now these companies – Ladbroke, Coral, Mecca, William Hill – were much more powerful than a little North Country lording; the Prime Minister had no interest in this vast and putrid chunk of British wealth and employment; and the minister responsible, a man whose name I've forgotten, was occupied with actresses; the Treasury was coldly unwilling to forego the Revenue's tax on betting on Johnny's behalf; and, after a miserable debate in the Lords at four in the morning, Johnny was left with a betting levy of three-quarters of a percentage point, deferred until 1990. At that moment, Newmarket and the racing pages remembered that Johnny had been excessively available to the press; that he was Left; that the bedroom floors at Wexley Park were quite cold and he didn't drink, absolutely nothing, and the food only so-so; that he quoted from Shakespeare; that he didn't shoot; that he'd retired the mare after two races, though she was rated by Timeform a stone better than Nijinsky; in short, that he was an utter shit, even by the standards of British racing, and had beaten up his first wife, that amazing girl Jane Haddon who's . . .

In this period, Johnny tried to remember his good fortune. For his marriage was also not prospering.

Candida was unlucky in the age she lived in. She was not educated, except in the sense that she had spent some years at schools in southern England; and her ignorance, which had not been a burden to her mother, was an unremitting anxiety to her. It had not occurred to her that she would have no idea of what interested her husband or that when, for example, Johnny and Stephen talked together, she would not understand what so concerned them; for a sense of her own raffishness, a slight insecurity in her Turpe-side social position, had caused her to pursue convention, to avoid ideas and scenes, and adopt the opinion of the majority at a time when the majority did not know what to think. Believing the Bellarmines to be the peak of her social world, and its embodiment in an extremity of refinement, authority and luxury, she had been dismayed by the ferment about her at Wexley Park, by Johnny's impatience with received ideas and his restlessness. She had never heard of Nathan Rothschild, so she did not know his wisdom: "It requires a great deal of boldness, and a great deal of caution, to make a great fortune; and when you have got it, it requires ten times as much wit to keep it." She didn't know that money comes into the world with a bloodstain on one cheek.

The house did not long occupy her. The mouldiest features of life at Wexley Park she quickly abolished; and, in truth, I fear I may have made a mistake in having beer and black pudding served at breakfast; and should have recognised that guests required a drink more stimulating than madeira so old it was the colour of hay and released in the glass, for a fugitive instant, the scent of a lost epoch. (Jane, of course, assumed that was normal fare in large family houses. Johnny, no doubt, approved his wife's reforms; and, anyway, he never criticised.)

Candida was less successful with her husband's Jane-era friends. Part of her nature approved Stephen: for hadn't he been the subject of a *Sunday Times* profile and made a fool of Paxman on *Newsnight*? Yet it infuriated her to come down with her letters to see him standing before the dining-room fire with his tankard and plate, damn him, for all the world as if he hadn't been drinking and raiding the kitchen and smoking his stuff till three. They could all go to gaol! To which Johnny said, "No doubt," and went solid, impregnable, in the way she hated. There's no't so stubborn as a Bellarmine. (Stephen himself was divided between a desire to provoke her (out of love for Jane) and to flatter her (out of love for Johnny). He cut a sorry figure.)

Candida's hostility to Stephen was natural; or rather it was a rational displacement from the actual target to whom she had sworn tremendous vows. Johnny broke her heart. She saw that nothing she could do could force him to reveal his feelings: that he didn't love her, yet came so close to counterfeiting love that nobody could detect the forgery; and that he could anticipate her anger, discomfort and desire. She felt abolished as a person and she saw, for a moment and with the most abject disgust, why Jane had behaved as she had. Such sympathy could not last. She decided that it was not Jane or Stephen who threatened her peace of mind – by which, I presume, she also meant the general social order she feared for – but the Bellarmines themselves in all their monstrous social arrogance, their religion and books and rituals of courtesy and kindness. What gave them the right to sit out the 1980s! (Another conclusion – that marrriage is intolerable to women and should not be entertained – was obscured from her by convention.)

I don't know when Johnny first became aware of Candida's unhappiness, which was the unhappiness of many Englishwomen of this period. I do know that by 1985, he saw that his great experiment had failed: that the abnegation and conformity of Candida were as doomed as the extreme bohemianism of Jane; and that all that remained was the working out of consequences and a disciplined decency until death relieved him. At first, he felt only anger at Jane for divorcing him. She'd taken with her a great piece of his vitality, and he'd retreated into a second marriage rather as his father, who'd had two commands sunk under him in the Indian Ocean, had retired to Northumberland after the war; and she'd so robbed him of his self-assurance that he'd accepted the world's judgement of Candida – of her prettiness, energy, impertinence – rather than trust his own heart. Sometimes alone at Wexley Park, when Candida was in London for some reason, he would walk the public rooms at night, and stare at Johnny and Meg by candle-light, or Omsai with his tattoos and powdered wig, and all the colonial governors and Presidents of the Board of Trade and heroes of the Turf, and feel his family's luck had departed; or rather, since he was not maudlin, that destiny and character, or luck and virtue, or whatever pairs you like to choose, were two sides of the same coin; were aspects of a metaphysical identity; and that it was his fault and his alone and his to make good. Having reached that conclusion, he cultivated a gaiety and kindness which the snobs approved and even Stephen felt to be instinctive or at worst the bad influence of Marcus Aurelius but were the results of Johnny's meditation on his fate.

His other job in 1985 and 1986 was as chairman of the Tyne & Wear Development Area. Johnny had an idea that the destruction of paid work in Newcastle in those years, which still reverberated so that men in the streets and supermarkets had a look of shock on them as if they'd been shot in the chest, was not inevitable, but rather an aberration, to do with credit policy or an overvalued exchange-rate or matters he had never really understood even when Jane had explained them to him; and that these men, of his generation or younger, had not suddenly lost their education and vigour but that, on the contrary, were desperate to exploit them. Johnny felt strongly about these things; and also that he was becoming ridiculous, even to Candida, who seemed to believe that these young men were somehow wicked and had got what they deserved. Johnny's support in '84 for Scargill, who had come to the house to talk about the Moresbydale pit but not stayed to lunch, was now seen by neighbours not as rebellion or hypocrisy, let alone as sympathy for the victims of history, but as pure daftness. That Johnny's predictions for the future of deep-coal mining – in an article for *The Times* that took him a week – were spectacularly borne out did him no good at all; for there is no virtue in being right before your time; a stopped clock is that; you must be right all the time, by changing, like a clock; and Johnny, once he had throught a question through, was generally satisfied to stay with his conclusion.

He led a trade mission to Tokyo. The councillors were drunk before the Channel, roaring in the aisles, upending boxes of steward's miniatures into Johnny's lap, while he smiled and cosseted. In Tokyo, he read in his room, because he thought his only value to the mission was his name and because the drinking bored him. He had a wish to visit Kyoto, because he'd read that it was beautiful, but didn't think he'd have time. On the third day, he was called down to the lobby where a young man with Eton English said, after an inordinate delay, that Mr Ashaguro would be happy to see Lord Bellarmine at the company retreat in Kyoto, between six and seven o'clock of Monday morning.

The garden, when he entered it, was of painful beauty under paper lamps. He thought that if he stumbled, or displaced a pine needle on the path or lit a cigarette (all of which he wanted to do) the place would detonate and vanish. Mr Ashaguro sat in a kimono on a mat just above Johnny, sometimes smiled, but said nothing at all during the interview which lasted four hours. For some reason, the young man now spoke French, and though Johnny spoke that language well because of his mother, he knew none of the technical terms in French of economics and the automobile industry.

He wanted to say: There is no shortage of capital or intelligence in England. Why the hell must we come to you to learn how to organise men and women in work, so that what they make is good and they are also happy? He prepared a polite version of this speech into good French but didn't say it, because it seemed such old hat in that garden. Johnny felt ashamed.

"Saito-*san* wishes to know which site you would have selected, Johnny-*san*."

Johnny dropped his head on to his chest. He thought for ten minutes, not that the passage of mere minutes mattered in that garden. A woman's voice beat maddeningly in his head: Not Sunderland, Mr Ashaguro, because the supplier base for a big industry like motor is atrophied in England; the domestic market is mature and anyway too small; also access to the continental market, which is, after all, what you need, is fragile. It is impossible to exaggerate the difference in mentality between England and Scotland and the continent. I'm not sure, from this distance, you've understood that, Mr Ashaguro. In Barcelona, at least, you have a domestic demand which is growing explosively, because of the belated modernisation of a country held back by Fascism; and also, a deep and enduring commitment to the European Community because it guarantees there will be no restoration of Fascism; and they all speak English, it's not a problem. I'd go for Barcelona, Mr Ashaguro.

Johnny didn't say that, not because Jane infuriated him in memory, though she did, but because he sensed that this thought was also, in some obscure way, available to Mr Ashaguro and the board of directors of Nissan. He said:

"Sunderland."

Mr Ashaguro was bathed in smiles.

The young man said in French: "This is also Saito-*san*'s wish."

Johnny stayed for another half-hour then took his leave. Against the wall of the garden, he smoked a cigarette until he noticed the cars and drivers, maybe a dozen of them, waiting to take him back to the capital. He went slowly through them till he found a radio telephone, and called Tom Burke, though it wasn't yet dawn in London, who woke fairly easily, kissed the young woman beside him on the bottom, and ran through the warm night to Downing Street where he found, not to his surprise, his princess working in her sitting room on the top floor.

She said: "You'll go for me, won't you, Tom. Now. If necessary with the RAF."

Tom's heart filled to bursting. He stood up, raking the ceiling with his head, and took a giant's step to the door, but she had something else to say.

"Who is Johnny Bellarmine?"

Tom was pierced with jealousy. He said, rather unwisely in the circumstances, "Was married to that girl Jane Haddon. Who runs . . ."

"Heavens," said the Prime Minister. "What on earth happened?"

Tom panicked. "I don't think he was very nice to her."

"Can't have been."

The Prime Minister shook her head, and returned to her papers.

Now Tom should have gone straight to Heathrow, for there was a British Airways flight to Tokyo at 8.15 and with availability. But he was excited, and feeling himself to be a gentleman, he felt he should first pay some of those small and intimate courtesies a gentleman devotes to a generous woman half his age before embarking on a long journey. While Mr Burke was engaged at his flat in these goodbyes, which needed an hour or even more than an hour, the Secretary of State was at his desk and heard, from a languid telephone call from Cabinet

Office, of his subordinate's commission and departure. This man, though of no intelligence or virtue, had great energy, and called Tom at home, countermanded the Prime Minister and halted the 747 at the end of runway five, to the unappeasable fury of Lord King of British Airways, till he himself could be delivered by limousine and Special Branch to loll on his three commandeered first-class seats.

Thus this investment, amounting to one thousand million pounds in capital and employing four thousand five hundred men directly and fifteen thousand at supplier businesses, was a triumph for the Secretary of State. In reality, of course, it was due ninety per cent to the skill and intelligence of the young men of Sunderland, five per cent to Johnny Bellarmine, four to Margaret Thatcher and one to Tom Burke; but for publicity and history, it was the whole and crowning work of a miserable nonentity I cannot even bear to name.

The consequence of all this, apart from some temporary prosperity where Tyne meets Wear and sea, was that Candida received a call from Downing Street, announcing that the Prime Minister and her consort and Mr Ashaguro and his officials would be staying at Wexley Park for the ground-breaking, if that were convenient. It was not. The staff panicked. The house turned upside down. Candida was pleased.

That evening, the Prime Minister patted the sofa beside her brilliant orange dress and, with a heart like lead, Johnny sat down. All the candles in both chandeliers had been lit, a procedure which had taken two estate workers in bibs the entirety of dinner. She offered him Minister of State at the Department of Trade and Industry – Tom could go to Transport – or Government Whip in the Lords. Johnny politely refused these honours and some others, for reasons he thought good but she simply would not understand: that he had not been elected by the people and therefore had no right to office of state; and, when that failed, that he was not a Tory and, indeed, but for the contradictions of his position and the prejudices of Walworth Road, would have been happy to sit as a Labour peer. Johnny twisted and turned in the brilliant candlelight, which sparkled in her beautiful eyes. He saw that she could not bear to be refused anything by a young man; that her will was stronger than his; and that, together with this implacable will, she could have her mind changed, a most unusual combination in woman or man. In the end, he agreed to write to her every week, even if he had nothing to say; and to chair a new Tyne & Wear Investment Authority, with five hundred million pounds in equity capital and its own borrowing authority, answerable to no Department but to a Cabinet-level committee. With that, it being one-thirty in the morning, the Prime Minister stood up, smiled to her somewhat hazy Denis, kissed Candida, shook the snoring Japanese and led the mightily relieved guests towards their bedrooms and sleep (or, in her case, just a spell at the boxes before bed).

At that moment, when Johnny's life began to compose into a conventional or brilliant career, when Candida spoke openly of babies, when he felt sometimes his head must burst with the poundings of his self-disgust, when he smashed a Newcastle baluster just to see the pieces on the fireplace marble; at that moment, Johnny had the incalculable good fortune to see his great ancestor in a dream; and recognised, that of all the manifold privileges of his life, this was the greatest.

8

In Bellarmine, a town in Alaska where young men in plaid shirts and caps with long peaks plough through the slush in pick-ups, there are two motels: the Best Western and the Days Inn. At the time in which we are interested, the first week of November, 1987, the Best Western had been block-booked by the oil company, and the Days Inn by Greenpeace, where they infiltrated each other's press conferences.

Stephen, to his great good fortune, sat next to a Fisheries Service biologist on the flight from Anchorage – the last, as it turned out, before the weather closed in – and this man lent him the use of his office at night. Stephen slept on a black plastic sofa under a Santa Fe blanket, pissed and brushed his teeth in the wash-room, and sometimes woke beside his fifth of Jack Daniel's and his tray of butts to secretaries calmly tapping about him and smiling: Morning, sunshine, bet you got a hard-on. Coffee's made.

At the Homestead each morning, where Stephen ate breakfast of caribou sausage and eggs, he saw a change come over the men from out of town, first slowly and then convulsively. Paul Stuart suits gave way to Gore-Tex and then plaid shirts and boots. Stubble sprouted on pale intellectual cheeks. Ira Rothenstein, of Maedel, Berliner, table-hopped in jeans and a baseball cap marked Grizzly River. Bill O'Donnell, of Cold Revett Spear, wore the T-shirt given him by one of the boys who'd come over the mountain looking for construction work: SAVE A LOGGER, SHOOT A SPOTTED OWL. It was soon established, first as a postulate, and then as case law, that those young men who had not yet found work would not be charged for their breakfast, but rather that the cost be compounded and billed to these great firms (or rather their clients, respectively the Zenon Corporation of New York and Greenpeace.) It was very merry, and Stephen wondered why all the world couldn't be like this where so many categories, old and young, west and east, Gentile and Jew, poor and rich, merged in the cold and long twilight.

Lunch and dinner he took at the same place, Marie's, a stand on the vacant lot behind the First Alaska Bank; and though sometimes he had mayonnaise with his bun of halibut steak, and sometimes ketchup, and sometimes coffee and sometimes Coke, it was not important; for he felt he could eat this ambrosial food every day of his life. The late evenings he spent in the impenetrable gloom of Suzanne's, admiring that lady's bosom and drinking Coors from the bottle, till it was three and Jane would be beginning at Burlington Street and he stood on line at the payphone under dripping supermarket eaves, cracking with partners in the slush; or sat on the plinth of Johnny Bellarmine's statue ringed by the boys dozing in their lit pick-ups, shared Marlboros or took his turn going for beer. Everybody, except the company and Greenpeace people, had taken up smoking: first Marlboros, and when those ran out, the generics used by the guys in construction. Ira Rothenstein, as the acknowledged *primus inter pares* of the New York liability bar, went further. Once, as he hustled the company blue suits into their hotel, he paused at the door and Stephen saw a jet of black tobacco juice shoot over his K-Mart shoulder, and gleam gloriously in the snow. There was a proposal to ration the Jack Daniel's till the weather cleared and the airport opened, but this was found, on examination, to be without merit.

The boat he found on the sixth day. It was steaming slowly up the sound. At the dock, the man was methodically securing ropes. He had come up from Seattle. His name was William.

"The summer rate is two hundred and fifty dollars a day. Never been up at this time of year." He looked round at the white peaks in intense satisfaction.

Since a cup of coffee at the Homestead now cost fifteen dollars, Stephen wondered if this charter rate would hold.

"How much you got, Stephen?"

"Five thousand five hundred," answered Stephen truthfully. This was no time for nickel-and-diming, one of many useful phrases Stephen had learned from his association with United States tort lawyers at the Homestead.

"Those French news people will pay two thousand a head."

"I'm easier cargo," said Stephen, putting out his hand.

"You got a ticket out, Stephen?"

"To Anchorage. I can get money there."

"How far you need to go?"

"As far as it takes."

"Five thousand a day or part of day. In cash. On the dock, prompt at midnight. You'll need a down jacket, a sleeping bag and food. I've got coffee. No liquor on board."

Stephen had never been on a boat of any description. He sat against the transom, in the down jacket he'd borrowed (or rather rented) from one of the guys, drinking coffee without cease, because it was American-strength and kept his hands warm. He liked the strange medium he was passing through, and the way the street-lights of Bellarmine receded ever so slowly in the distance. He chain-smoked so as to have something to smell.

As they passed through the Narrows – he sensed wet granite walls at each side – a buoy bell tolled drearily, as three sea-lions squabbled and shifted position on it. William turned and smiled. From the boat's light, and the sound, he saw they were passing through blocks of putrid ice which hissed and crackled.

"Brash," said William, speaking for the first time.

The sun came up fast on a landscape more beautiful than Stephen had ever seen or could possibly have imagined: towering white mountains and glaciers falling steeply into a deep green sea. Then the sun vanished into the low cloud. A little later, William pointed to the first rainbow swirls on the calm surface; then they passed into a brownish-white mousse that blew up in their wash and danced like detergent foam across the water. William fished out a dead bird, which he cleaned with a rag and pronounced a murre: he laid it on newspaper, in case the San Diego people wanted an autopsy. They passed the *Zenon Bellarmine* a mile away on the port beam, listing badly, the hole in its side gaping. Two Coast Guard cutters stood by, paying out an orange boom. William shook his head.

Two hours further on, Stephen saw a sight so strange it might have fallen out of a dream. On a stony island beach, young people in orange protective suits were seated in rows, polishing stones with rags and, when they'd finished, tossing them back into the viscous black water. William said: "I guess they think, if they put the whole county on the payroll, they'll get off light."

"I want to land, William."

"Suit yourself. You'll break your fucking legs."

Which Stephen almost did: he simply could not get a purchase on the rocks, and fell repeatedly, tearing his jeans and bloodying both knees. He found a girl, who smiled at him, and said they were under instructions from the company not to talk to press.

"Fuck you, William," said Stephen.

"It's OK."

The water was now so thick, that it seemed to crease on the bow, and Stephen smelled something foul: probably sulphur, since this was crude oil. They no longer stopped for birds, which were just disturbances in the surface tension of the oil, or for the big fish, which William said were Chinook salmon. Stephen was sick over the stern-board and William brought him some whisky from the cabin.

"I thought you said the boat was dry," said Stephen through gobs of sick.

But William was gaping over Stephen's shoulder. He reached for the big fish-tailer, that he carried for the Chinook clients, and hauled something out of the water. It was about four feet long, moving its head spastically from side to side in the sling.

"Watch it, Stephen. He'll take your face . . ."

But it was too late. As Stephen grabbed for the hind legs, the animal turned on him with a ferocity he'd never witnessed. His down jacket ripped the length of his arm, spilling kapok and blood and shocking pain.

"Get the fucking legs," shouted William.

Stephen caught them, slithered, and caught them again and busied himself with his pain. Black watery shit poured on his hands.

William had it by the back of the head. It was hissing anger and black vomit. He was saying, "Don't lick your fur, you dumbfuck, that's what's killing you, you fucking jerk."

"We can turn, William. If you think it'll make it back."

"Live, you bastard, live!" And then, more quietly, "You dumb jerk. You fucking dumb jerk."

Stephen could feel the strength going out of the hind legs, and all the wildness and strangeness, draining away, till they were just two sticks in his hands, cold and oily.

William put the dead sea-otter down on the newspaper, and knelt down and started rubbing it with rags.

"I think we should go back now, William."

William got up, went into the cabin for the First Aid, cleaned Stephen's arm with Dettol and Neosporin and gave him a tetanus injection in the other arm. Then he engaged the engine, and turned about in the thick sea.

They didn't speak till they were out of the slick, and past the island, where the people were gone, taken out maybe by helicopters, and the mousse and the tanker, listing on their starboard bow, still pouring out six thousand barrels an hour. By now, Stephen was trembling uncontrollably, and they shared some soup, and Stephen had some more Jack Daniel's, and warmed up. The mountains were rose in the late twilight.

"You know why Bellarmine is called Bellarmine? Why that boat's called what it is?"

Stephen nodded. Oh yes, Second Voyage, looking for the North-West Passage, the statue's a copy of the one in Newcastle.

"Came up here in the summer of 1775, the year of the Concord fight, you know, the Shot Heard Round the World . . ."

Stephen nodded.

"Looking for the Passage. They tested for salinity by lowering wine bottles off the stern and tasting the sea water. Coming through the

Narrows, it began to taste sweet, so he turned about and sailed down the Sound, named it Prince William Sound after some royal guy you had . . ."

"The King's son . . ."

". . . right, and then turned north and discovered what's now Anchorage."

William slowed the engine. The water roared past them, but they stayed put between the wet black walls. He said: "He just came and went. You'd never know he'd ever been through here with two stern-riggers. He didn't destroy a fishery that fed a thousand families, or kill two hundred thousand birds and God knows how many sea mammals like that otter. He just came and when he saw that there was no passage through, he turned about. What's wrong with us now? What are we doing to this country?"

"How much, William?"

He started up the engine, slowly. "For the economic damage, I guess one billion dollars. And for the . . . for the . . ." He couldn't find a word.

"Insult?"

"Right. For the insult: well, this state always hated the oil companies, they were so damn arrogant, filled the Inuit with whisky and bought up State congressmen so they could get the pipeline right of way down from the North Slope. And even so, the State Legislature said the tankers must have double hulls for the Sound. Did that vessel appear to you to have a double hull, Stephen?"

"No, sir."

"So, for the insult: four billion dollars. Is that what you're hearing, Stephen? Five billion dollars."

"That's what I'm hearing."

He could see the glow of Bellarmine against the peaks behind, when he said: "You know his descendant is my friend."

William looked at him over his shoulder. William found clients liked to brag out in the boat: as if the different medium had its own rules of evidence and propriety.

"Oh yes. What's his name, your friend?"

"Johnny Bellarmine."

For some reason, this answer satisfied William. But he was not much of a talking man. He just said: "You gonna tell him what you've seen here?"

"Yes."

"You do that." He inhaled. "Going to be fine tomorrow."

Stephen said nothing. He was looking at the glow of Bellarmine or rather at the thought that had interposed itself between him and the street-light. The thought was formal, shapely, declaratory, complete, for it was phrased not just in the present but in the future and the past. It was that the harbour from which he'd set out, and to which he was now returning, was loneliness: a loneliness that had been so much of his life for so long he hadn't been aware there might be other conditions of existence; and was, he now saw, indistinguishable from his optimism, or rather the certainty that for all his melancholy and scruple, he'd come, in the end, to the top of his generation and do some good. The thought congealed on him, cold and tight as the white peaks in the soaring air-pressure, or the scab of blood on his arm. He knew also, and with the same certainty, as certain as the harbour dancing towards him on the black waves and the snow swirling in the slow headlights by the refinery, that his loneliness and hope were created at the same instant of his past but only now had taken a shape he could apprehend; and that was the instant the stained-glass door closed on his father's raincoat, for the sound at last had reached him, burst on him in a boom and a rattling of panes, that reverberated off the steel mountains and black sea, round and round and round and would go on ringing in his ears for so long as he lived. Stephen put his hands to his ears, and whispered, Everything you lost I found, everything you sold I bought and kept for you; but it was too late for that; or rather that its irony and self-pity would not do any more now his life was beginning, not for Johnny ("You're Cohen, aren't you? I'm . . .") and not for Dad. Stephen put his hands to his face, in case the thought – the first in his life– destroy his optimism.

They came into the harbour at three a.m.

Stephen said: "You'll have to take my IOU for the second day. I'll wire the money from Anchorage to your account, if you give me the number and the bank routing number."

William shook his head. "You gave me a tad too much." He handed Stephen ten oily hundred-dollar bills, and that was a good thing, because Stephen needed to replace the jacket, and get his arm stitched and eat something. As the nurse at Bellarmine Methodist worked expertly with her needle, Stephen felt a sadness that this last memento of a wild thing, of a thing that was not human or under human power, would also vanish.

Every two or three months, Jane had a dream of the first summer she spent with Johnny at his house. At that time Jane, as a courtesy to Lady Bellarmine and her old-fashioned ways, slept in the bedroom at Wexley Park known as The Cliff. She'd see light race over the carpet and then retreat. Hear the window blind rattle and then be still.

May I sleep in your bed, Jane?

Yes, sir, you may.

The ring of her water glass. The crackle of linen. His coldness. The superfluity of nightgowns.

Still composed in sleep, she feels the warm cotton on her face, his weight on her thigh, her unencumbered breast. As her senses open like petals, her breast sings, her waist turns to ocean, she knows she must move or die. But as her body convulses, she wakes and hears traffic and telephones and barge horns from the Elbe, and sees that this is not Johnny and The Cliff but the Atlantic Hotel in Hamburg, and the phone ringing and the smell of last year's cigarettes and her nightgown at her armpits, and the weight of her wrist on her groin; and misery bursts from her hips and mouth and eyes.

At these times, Jane knows that whatever the purpose of life, it isn't happiness and she'll have trouble making her three score and ten.

The phone rang and rang. Jane picked it up.

"Jane!" The voice was full of cold and streetlight. "Why can't you answer the fucking phone?"

"I'm sorry, Stephen. I was fast asleep."

"What are you doing in fucking Germany anyway?"

"I've a meeting with Hartmann." This old man was a well-known German clothing manufacturer, and a valued supplier to R & S.

94

"I've seen it, Jane! I got a boat at last, went down the Sound today. I can't describe it."

"Try."

"Jane, it's a five-six fucking billion dollar claim. The company's running about without a head. They're completely out of their depth. They're going to be taken to the cleaners by every damn fisherman in Alaska, by the State and every crummy agency of the Federal Government. I've just seen Jack Pollack of the company and he says they're filing a declaratory suit against their insurers. And Goddam Ira's handling it . . ."

The alterations in Stephen's manner, the deterioration in his language and his new familiarity with famous names, struck Jane vaguely, but she had not the imagination to reconstruct their causes. She said:

"If that is the case, your friend is ruined. Actually, the whole Lloyd's market is."

"What the fuck are you talking about, Jane?"

"You'll need to take over the syndicates yourself, Stephen. I'll help you as much as I can."

"What?"

"You see, I don't think anybody at that place is capable of doing it. You'll have to close them out into new syndicates, Stephen, under your management. And run them off over five to ten years."

"You're mad, Jane. I'm not becoming a fucking underwriter at Lloyd's."

"You won't be. You won't underwrite any more insurance. You'll merely pay off the claims."

Out in the Peri-Arctic, Stephen felt for the first time the scale of Jane's audacity and self-confidence; and also something else, something vast, that up to that point had been outside his experience; as if she were an ice-berg, nine-tenths submerged from view.

He cupped his hand over the mouthpiece: "Excuse me, guys, could you step back a little, I have a very, very sensitive business matter to discuss."

"Sure, Steve."

"You want a beer, Steve?"

"Please."

"Jane, are you there?"

"I'm here, Stephen."

"If the syndicates stop writing new business, there'll only be claims to honour and costs and salaries to pay and no cash coming in to pay it. What if the new syndicates declared bankruptcy, just walked away from the storms and Bellarmine and the Old Years, or settled at twenty-five cents to the dollar? Jane?"

After a while, she said: "I think that would be the end of the City. And of the country, really. I think it would be better to find a source of reliable cash flow to fund the syndicates' liabilities."

"But I've got no fucking capital."

"So you'll have to go to Martin."

"For God's sake, Jane! You're fucking dreaming."

"I was. Not now. You need a cheap and reliable source of cash flow over a ten-year period. What's the cheapest source of profits in the stock market, Stephen?"

"Tobacco, I guess."

"Well, you must buy a medium-sized tobacco company. Tobacco's a very good business, Stephen. You make it for a penny, sell it for a dollar, and it's addictive. It's the happiness of many poor people."

"That's a repellent way to talk, Jane. It's a killer. I'm not going to help one person at another's expense."

"There is that. More to the point, Stephen, if tobacco really is lethal, as most people seem to think it is, at some stage the industry will be destroyed by liability suits arising from its own product. Martin will know. But you'll have to go straight to Los Angeles. I don't think he's got much longer."

"He won't even take my fucking call!"

"Yes, he will. Give me five minutes and I'll warn them."

"Jane, you are the most conceited person I have ever met; also the most devoted . . ."

"Well, I wouldn't exaggerate, Stephen. You asked me to help you and it's no great bother. German hotel beds are very hard, so I never sleep well here. And you're right. It's been good for us. You showed good judgement and also humanity. Good night, Stephen."

"Good night, Jane," said Stephen, feeling five-six billion dollars.

"You done, Steve?"

"Just one more. Won't take a second."

As Stephen had feared, Martin did not take his call. He listened to the drips from the eaves for a minute, and then Donna was back on. She said: "Marty will see you for ten minutes at 3.50 a.m. on Sunday, November 10. No lawyers, associates or smoking. Do you know where we are?"

"Yes," said Stephen.

"Say hi! to your principal from us. Is it cold up there, Steve?"

"Yes, but so beautiful it sings in the imagination, Donna."

"Sounds neat."

Looking up, Stephen saw stars all over the sky.

That day, Alaskan Airways laid on six flights. They came in empty from Anchorage and left full. Stephen got out on the fourth. He thought, as he queued, clean-shaven, among the suits: Principal, is it, you cow! And then, a bit later: Oh yes, very clever. Cow! There was no smoking on the flight, since that is a FAA regulation for short-haul flights within the US, and the drinks were soft. Nobody talked. Stephen thought: What I do for you, Captain Johnny Bellarmine! The other passengers were, if Stephen had only known it, thinking similar thoughts though free of that accursed irony: invoking not perhaps the Great Navigator, or his descendants by blood and marriage, but a voracious building on Water Street or a daughter at Princeton or a retirement village in Sarasota, Florida, and with a regret that all but stopped their hearts.

He flew to Los Angeles by way of Portland and San Francisco.

Marty's 3.40 ran over two minutes, so Stephen felt curiously powerful as he entered the big room. Four clean desks, with phones and computer monitors on them, met at the centre, where Martin was seated, completing a telephone call. The blinds were drawn on the warm Beverly Hills night. As Stephen came in, young men and women in casual clothes unwound themselves and converged on the cross of desks, and perched on them or stood, smiling at him with undivided attention.

"Hi, Steve," said Martin, replacing the telephone and turning on his chair.

Stephen sensed an infinitesimal slowness in his movement; as if he were weary; as if he felt something closing in on him and he must lift his head, look out at the world, at things he'd never considered: counsel, public affairs advice, personal security, maybe even a rabbi. He sensed that Martin's unbelievable power, his faith and credit greater than Zenon or the Morgan Bank, greater even than the Federal Reserve, greater even than John Law or Nathan in their primes, so that just a phone call to the AP-Dow Jones tape that Handel & Wind was highly confident of raising funds for such acquisition was enough to detonate a corporation the size of a country, was ebbing away; was, in itself, not to be tolerated on the earth, let alone in an insomniac Jewish boy with too much money and no character in California; and the people smiling at him in the artificial light had not understood this, so mesmerised were they by Martin's genius.

Stephen said: "She needs to help a friend who has unfunded insurance liabilities at Lloyd's of London. We can't get a handle on the full extent, but we're working with a figure for all the syndicates of a hundred million dollars ten years out, discounted to present value at four per cent."

"Why the low cap rate?" said somebody.

Marty raised a hand.

"The liabilities are ninety per cent in dollars, so she needs a US business that'll earn profits after capital spend, financing and taxes of fifteen to twenty million dollars in year one; and will not generate its own future insurance liabilities."

"Sounds like GenCo, Marty."

Marty spoke. He said: "Does Jane like hostile?"

"Not hostile."

"Will she invest?"

"Her net worth."

"Do management?"

"Non-executive chairman. She's a bad air traveller."

Marty sighed. He said: "There's a property out of Bradenton, Iowa, makes . . ."

". . . pre-sifted biscuit dough, name of Clabber Lady." A young black woman took up the story. "Caretaker management. Family wants to sell. Fiscal '86 net earnings of twelve point five million dollars. I guess it's a liquidation."

Stephen nodded.

Marty said: "We'll do a mixture of Zeroes and Pay-in-Kind. New York will handle the tender offer . . ."

"Not New York," said Stephen.

"Maybe Steve and Donna . . ."

The young woman gleamed at the opportunity.

Marty began to turn his chair. He said, over his shoulder: "The firm's fee is fifteen per cent of the equity, five per cent of the transaction."

"We're talking piety here, Marty. I'm not taking a fee."

The young people shuddered. The room seemed to fill with bad American vowels: Harlem, New York; Decatur, Georgia; Chicago South Side; the San Fernando Valley. They shrieked: Who is this British jerk?

But Stephen, because of his recent education, knew.

A man said: "Who is this sleaze Jane's bailing out?"

Marty glared at him in fury. Stephen saw that the man, with his unbusinesslike intervention, had cost the Beverly Hills office of Handel & Wind several tens of millions of dollars; and because money was the touchstone of these people's lives, the measure of their achievement, because they had not passed beyond it, not even Martin, that was bad.

"OK, Steve. Five and one. You'll have fun with Donna. Say hi to Jane from us."

In the outer office, Stephen was worshipped to his briefcase. He noted his audience had lasted eight minutes. Martin was back on schedule. Not that it would save him.

Stephen and Donna did have fun, lounging at airline counters, in the air, in Bradenton in meetings with family and management, and in downtown Los Angeles at counsel's office, going through the tender offer line by line; but this pleasure was purely intellectual, arose in the clash and resolution of their intelligences, to the great sadness of the lady, who found Steve kind of cute. For Stephen had been thinking on his business trip, and had come to the understanding that fidelity, far from being a virtue among virtues, was the greatest of them all, the virtue of virtues; though he was sad, too, for he loved her gaiety, and ignorance, and quickness of mind, and amazingly beautiful colour.

One endless night, Stephen returned to London for he also had business there.

"Can I come in, Lizzie?"

She looked, not flustered, but composed; and, for the first time in their long association, Stephen realised she had an existence independent of his perception of it. She stood back, and let him pass through the stained-glass sunlight into her doll's-house drawing room. She came in behind him, and made for her tray of bottles and glasses, as if to offer him a drink: as if she still sensed the vestige of a routine.

"Lizzie, I want to say something to you. It might be a good idea for you to sit down."

The words arrested her in mid-movement, and Stephen saw, in this space between conventional pictures of her, her green and perfect girlishness.

"I'm afraid, Lizzie, I am going to stop seeing you. This is because I'm not sure I love you but I do love Jane Bellarmine, and have done ever since I first saw her. I think there's a falseness here, which if it goes on, will eventually prevent me knowing what true is."

Lizzie did not move. Her eyes were still on the drinks tray.

Whatever Stephen had expected, he had not expected this. He said:

"I'd like to give you a present. I was short on Wall Street on Black Monday, and made some money: actually, quite a large sum of money, actually. I would like to give it to you, if you'll let me."

Lizzie stirred, completed her step; then turned to look at him. Her eyes were black with hatred.

She said: "I don't want your money or you. Please leave, now."

At that moment, Stephen knew he'd made a mistake. He saw that he'd never looked at her, never listened to her, in all their love affair. He saw that if once, just once in those eighteen years, between Apsos in Cyprus and Sternwood Road in Chiswick, he'd said to her: "What do *you* think, Lizzie?" she'd have opened like a bud in spring; and so, eventually, would he. And now their positions were reversed, it was all too late, and a great piece of his life – in the future, no doubt, but no less solid and luxurious to the imagination and sweet to the taste and touch – had shivered into a million million pieces. And he thought: Time to grow up, my man, else you'll do yourself an injury.

He wanted to say something more, but could see it better be short, or she'd hit him, hard, in the eyes or balls, or pick up something that would bruise or cut. He said his thanks and left; and found himself a half-hour later, and much to his surprise, back at the airport.

9

Needing to read the epistle in Wexley church and not finding his mother's prayer book, Johnny went into the library to see if there was another. He did find one, on a high shelf. It was bound in boards of narwhal horn, with a small golden cross inlaid in the ivory on front and back. He began to tremble so the steps shook, and he descended. In the inside of the back board was some eighteenth-century handwriting. It wasn't hard to read:

> Latitude 70° 18' South Longitude 115° 38' West Furthest South Nov. 15th 1767
>
> The *Good Hope* being near beset in the Ice, and Anxious that such a Condition not befall the lighter Vessel, we turned about and beat for the Cape, making good time. I who had Ambition not only to go farther than any one had done before, but as far as it was possible for man to go, was not sorry at meeting with this Interruption as it in some measure relieved us, at least shortened the dangers and hardships inseparable with Navigation at High Latitudes. For God, in His inestimable Wisdom, has resolved not yet to call us to His Mercy, but has prepared for us some Enterprise to be Completed for His Glory. And I was filled with Joy that He had seen Fitt to show me my death. For when it pleases Him, we shall come again to this Place, and steer between these Wrecks of a Shatter'd world till we anchor at last beneath a warm Wind-shore.

Johnny felt an overwhelming strangeness, as if he had swallowed poison. For the first time in years, for as long as he could remember, he was interested: not as a display to please or amuse or console, or for reasons of leadership or subordination or pious social usefulness, but in the core of his nature. Something here concerned him not as dutiful son or loving husband or embodied estate, as figure of envy or fun, but as a man born in a particular moment with a particular composition: the handwriting was his private business and his alone. He had, he understood with a sort of shudder, felt this sense of privacy as a child, and then again in the novelty and sweetness of his first love affair at university; but not since. His excitement mounted to the point he had to pace the room. He tried to imagine the innumerable pathways of blood, accident, instruction and will that had caused his career to cross that of his immortal ancestor; and of the immense, almost boundless, possibilities that arose from that concidence. It was as if two planes of reality had intersected, a crossing he sensed was neither providential nor appropriate nor likely to be repeated, but an event all the same: a point of departure, a moment at which his life could begin. He was conscious, again for the first time, that his life did not need to be as it was; could indeed take any shape he wished for it; and could, in its boldness and vigour, emulate even that of his ancestor. And now, amid his excitement, Johnny felt a regret that he had not discovered this message earlier in his life, when his spirit was still strong and his optimism intact; and immediately this regret lost its passivity, began to catch and flame and roar till it was an uncontrollable rage at his first wife, that junkie bitch, that daughter of a whore.

He was still angry with Jane, five days later, on the windy airstrip at Punta Arenas in Chilean Patagonia, as he stared with interest at the 1956 DC-6 which would be his transport south. Charlotte Meredith, sister of the airline's founder, was talking to him, technically. Candida had elected not to come, not wishing perhaps to camp for an unspecified period on the Polar Plateau, eat frozen tortillas and turkey cooked in Vegemite every day, piss in a barrel, go mad with panic in a whiteout, die in a crevasse; and perhaps she felt she could profit from a husband's absence.

Johnny was still angry, fourteen hours later, as the aircraft shuddered and began its base leg. The Independence Hills lurched in from the left, the cross-winds drawing great plumes of snow from off the summits like the hair in equestrian paintings of Napoleon. A line of oil drums, ballasted with urine, plunged and righted itself below. Johnny's stomach jumped in his ribs, his anger flew out of his mouth, and as he whispered, Look, he saw the yawing ice below was blue as the Mediterranean; and as that thought came in and stuck, they hit the ground, a seat broke loose and sailed for the bulkhead, the windows roared and spouted with snow, the passengers were whooping with applause, they were bouncing on rooftops; at that moment, Johnny Bellarmine felt a deathly sadness to be here without Jane, to be on the last continent among strangers, but the door was being manhandled open, blasts of sunlight baffled him, the engines shrieked, a girl in a parka was pulling herself into the blinding doorway, shouting:

"Which one is Johnny? You've got a window, Johnny. Clear to the Pole. But you've got to go now. Now! Please be very, very careful on the blue ice. Hi, everybody! I'm Janet! From Christchurch, New Zealand! Welcome to sunny . . ."

Johnny hated the way they helped him down the companionway and how, when he pushed them off, he slipped and fell on the ice. He hated the sunshine and the unbelievable cold and the running and the two men shrieking in his ears and the tail of the Twin Otter pitching before him and the burst of its engines as it fired up above him; but what let tears into his eyes and panic into his gut was that, turning, he saw the DC-6 take off; so little beneath the towering mountains; slow and desperate, like a pensioner climbing stairs; till it passed behind the Independence Hills on its long journey back to Latin America.

Johnny flew for nine hours, bent double among the spare fuel tanks and survival rations, looking out through a tiny square of window at the shadow of the aircraft skidding over the snow ridges. He dined off splintered crackers and frozen Chilean Gouda passed down to him in the engineer's mittened palm. Every hour or so, he relieved himself into the spout of a plastic can marked "Avgas Only" while speculating coyly about what Jane or Mrs Meredith would do in such circumstances. He stared at the skipping shadow: numb, speechless, miserable and deaf.

The Pole bored Johnny, and he was cold as he had never been in his life. (On 15 January, 1986, the reading at Amundsen-Scott South Pole Station was minus thirty-five degrees Fahrenheit, with another minus fifteen degrees Fahrenheit of wind-chill, though it warmed a little later in the day.) His British boots might have been ballet shoes for all the cold they kept out. The Americans were officially hostile, and unofficially like pests. They gave a party for him after work in the part of the base called Summer Camp. Johnny sipped commissary whisky, at a cost, he imagined, to the people of the United States of at least five dollars a swallow in Avgas alone, while the girls – astrophysicists, cosmic ray specialists, waste managers – scalded him with desire: so that, for the first and only time in his life, he said he had to piss, and opening the hut flap on the incandescent midnight, left without saying goodbye. The pilots were doing cross-words in the fuselage, and smiled at him shyly, as if to say: Everybody has to do it once. He pitched his tent without their help and crawled into his sleeping bag.

But whether it was the whisky or the lady scientists or the altitude or the cold, or his clinging thermal underwear, something gave him a longing for Jane that he knew he couldn't master. And since he was sure he hadn't flown twelve thousand miles to jerk off, he got up and started walking down the ski-way the Americans had made for the Navy Hercules that resupplied them every morning; but thoughts of Jane pursued him like the sun-dogs and, as he trudged over the sastrugi, reluctantly, wearily, he let them in.

"Jane, I have to work!"

She recoiled from him to the extremity of her side of the bed. As he got up, he pulled himself together. He said: "Would you like me to get a TV?"

"No, why?"

"Jane, I have to do my bloody essay. That will take me at least four hours and possibly all night."

"I'll just wait here. I mean, if that's all right."

His heart dissolved. "Jane, you should work, too, you know. You've got to make your way in the world, however clever you are."

"I go to all my lectures."

"But what about your essays or whatever you have."

"I did it, this morning."

Ah, thought Johnny. This is my girlfriend's degree work: standing at the chest of drawers in her night-gown, hair in her mouth, with three pieces of paper and a biro, and occasionally rubbing the calf of one bare leg with the instep of another; a bit of scribbling on one paper; and then, with intense concentration, a fair copy, her tongue peeking between her lips; the whole procedure occupying a full ten minutes, one day a week.

"I wonder, Jane, if you shouldn't type your answers."

"I don't know how to type."

"I do. I'd like to do it for you."

Which he did, every week; and though he never touched the calculations, he made some alterations, with the aid of a dictionary, to sense and orthography.

"Shouldn't we go out, Jane?"

"Where?"

"To a pub or something."

She looked doubtful.

"It's fun."

"Someone might see us."

"They might, Jane."

She said nothing.

"Look, Jane, we're not breaking the law. You're over sixteen, for God's sake!"

She said nothing.

They went to a well-known pub on the river. Jane looked fit to burst with pleasure. He brought her some more beer and said, when he sat down beside her on the step:

"Tell me about your family and Glasgow and everything."

"I don't want to, and if you ask me again, I'll leave and not come back."

"I won't."

A bit later: "Are you still cross with me, Jane?"

"Why should I be? I love you."

"Don't be so daft!"

"You're the daft one."

"Hey, Johnny!"

"Heavens! Johnny invite someone to stay! I never thought to hear those words from you."

They were lunching at her London house.

"And what's his name? Or her name?" she said archly.

"Jane. She does maths at Somerville. She's very nice."

"And does Jane have a surname?"

"No she does not. She has a name, Haddon, but it's not her real name."

"Ah," said Elizabeth Bellarmine, more to herself than her son.

"Oh for God's sake, Mum!"

She looked up. "Would it help you if I wrote to Miss Haddon at Somerville?"

"It would help me very much."

Johnny!

Johnny saw the letter often. It said in part:

> I would be delighted to have you with us, for the whole vacation, if you would like that. My son says you are a good scholar, and that pleases me greatly. I never saw the point of going to Oxford except to learn. I am very proud of his Studentship, and no doubt that is in some measure due to your example. His father got a Pass degree, and I never went, because girls didn't in those days.

I have asked them to make ready for you a bedroom we
have here called The Cliff, which has a view of the sea that
some people have enjoyed. There is a small sitting room
where you can work, if you need to.

I do not expect a reply, but look forward to meeting you
on the 16th,

Yours sincerely
Elizabeth Bellarmine

Johnny smiled at the recollection of his mother's officiousness, though
he had been embarrassed. Jane didn't seem to notice, and was very
pleased with the letter, taking it around with her, often re-reading it.

For God's sake, Johnny!

He opened his eyes. He saw the engineer's terrified face. He was
carrying a pair of long felt boots. Behind him was a moving airplane,
like a dog on a leash. Johnny stopped walking.

"You're frost-bit, Johnny. Charlotte will carve us up. You never,
never, go anywhere without the VHF. Or we kill you. Do you
understand?"

Johnny nodded.

"It's twelve thousand feet up, here. Let's see your feet."

Johnny sat down on the snow.

"Left is bit, not badly. You can check your dick yourself. Try these."

Johnny's feet were engulfed in blessed warmth.

"Red-Army issue. Use them in Siberia. Scammed them at
Komsomolskaya."

Johnny said: "I'll look after them and return them to you. I won't
forget this kindness, Andy."

"It's nothing. Let's go. The weather's clear as a bell. Walt wants to
show you something. On the house."

They flew for a day. Johnny dozed and was jolted awake, to the aircraft
racing down under sheer cliffs of ice and, through his scrap of window,
a sight that might have fallen from another world: thousands on

thousands on thousands of, sweet heaven!, penguins, more numerous than the souls of the dead in Homer, streaming towards him. The ground came up to meet him and he saw Andy, tumbling out on to the snow like a parachutist on landing and, as they climbed and wheeled, shaking out a big Canadian flag and swirling it over his head as he ran to clear the birds while the Otter came down and bumped and bounced along behind him.

Johnny fell down the steps and reached the ground at precisely the moment the first of the penguins reached him. They came up close, gabbling questions at his chest. Who are you? What is your country? Where is your mate? Do you feel cold? Are these boys your brothers? Do you care for krill? Do you also incubate your egg on your feet? Johnny stood up, but this sent the birds scattering, so he knelt down and they ran back. And Johnny, alone with Walt and Andy, among approximately forty-one thousand Emperor penguins,* thought: O Lord, that I have lived to see this miracle.

"My brothers!" he cried, his arms out wide and high above his head. "My friends!"

What are you saying? How do you speak? What is this big red thing you came in? Please answer?

But Andy was running the engines, and Walt, in a tuxedo for the photograph, was pointing hard at the aircraft and they were up again and climbing, banking over the running penguins who raised a tumult of distress and, if this can be possible, offence; and Johnny felt their sorrow engulf him.

The pilot was also moved. He screamed: "They're something else, those damn birds, something else." Then, about an hour later: "Independence's closing up. White-out. Damn penguins."

Ah, thought Johnny. Novelty.

"Can we make the Pole?"

Thumb down.

"*Teniente O'Leary?*"

Thumb down.

* Korf and Palmström Census, 1980.

"The Russians?"

Thumb down.

"I am extremely sorry, Walt, Andy."

"Don't be. It's been fun."

They flew for a bit, going nowhere in particular, their shadow skipping along the ice. Johnny thought: It is, in a sense, an exemplary way to go. We are sustained in this medium by intelligence, which must fail. We must fall to earth.

Then the pilot whooped: "*Belgrano's* been on. There's fuel at Foundation. Argentine Air Force. Air drop."

"What's Foundation?"

"A place."

A white place. A flat place ringed in the immense distance by shining peaks. A place with a tiny red stain, which was six lashed fuel drums all but covered in snow, and a tall whipping cane topped by the flag of Argentina, and the remains of a parachute harness. Swirls of crevasses, like hairs on an albino dog. A glacier place.

The engineer squeezed half-way into the cabin, and screamed in Johnny's ear. "OK, we've got Avgas for four passes. You get to hang out the airplane. On the third. If you're lucky."

The first pass was at about ten feet. As far as Johnny could tell, the snow looked perfect, with low sastrugi up to about six inches. The second time, the shadows touched, the skis fizzed on the snow, smooth as water. Then they climbed abruptly, Andy wriggled through, pulled back the cabin door, and took his client, who had paid forty thousand dollars in cash for his holiday, firmly by the feet.

The cold and sunshine hit Johnny like a drawn sword. They came in at about five feet along the ski-track, very fast. Johnny was looking for gashes across the track, where snow bridges had broken or partly collapsed. The track was clean, about a foot deep all its length into the sastrugi, straight as time, lovely. The engineer pulled him in as they climbed.

Thumb up.

Suddenly, the cabin filled with radio. It was not Independence, but Punta: Mrs Meredith, on the High Frequency. "Johnny," she wailed, "Johnny . . ." She vanished into the ionosphere. Her Scots made her sound like Jane. She'd never lost a client in seven years, only her brother.

"OK, belt up, guys," shouted the pilot happily. "No smoking etcetera. FAA regulations etcetera. I am now going to land this airplane. Nice knowing you, Mr Johnny."

"Sweet mother Mary, mother of God, intercede with your blessed son, our Lord Jesus, son of God . . ." The engineer was of Polish origin.

The aircraft dived for the snow. The wheel-skis hit their shadows, which merged, separated, merged again. Roaring of engines smashed into reverse. The hiss of skis.

" . . . sweet mother of God, intercede for us with your blessed son, our only God . . ."

Spirit of the penguins, be with us now and at . . .

The nose plunged, then rose again. The tail came down, bounced, settled. The aircraft stopped. The engines shut down. It was quiet.

"I am one fucking great genius aviator," the pilot whispered.

"Evidently," said Johnny.

"Bullshit," said the engineer, who was crying.

As he got out, Johnny looked past the tail, and saw, across the tracks of the wheel-skis, a chasm like the mouth of death.

The pilot stood by him like a ghost. "Only the fucking Argentine military would drop in a fucking crevasse field!"

With difficulty, Johnny turned to look at him. "If there's something to pay for the fuel, I'll pay it. Do you understand, Walt?"

"I don't think so, Johnny. It's ours or nobody's. I don't think this place will ever let another airplane down."

They spent many days at Foundation Glacier; and many nights, or rather pieces of the treadmill sunshine during which Walt and Andy snored in red bell-tents. Since there was a time difference of seventeen hours between Independence Hills and the Pole, they could not even set their watches. They were out of time. During the waking time, they worked on a ski-way, probing the snow with ski-poles and the flag cane, while, in the warm, almost zero, air, the crevasses cracked like rifle shots around them: like, as Andy said in amazement, the woods at home in hunting season. Johnny cooked for them from the survival rations, since they didn't know how. They had six bottles of an Argentinian liquor called *Pisco* which the pilots drank doused in Coke, but Johnny took with just a piece of immemorial ice that he cut from under the snow, at a place he knew no man or animal had been in all time, with his Swiss Army knife and brought back fizzing in a Chinese thermos. He decided alcohol was all right, in small quantities, in pleasant company. On the first day, Mrs Meredith came over the High Frequency.

"I called Washington, Johnny. I called the Navy. Immediately."

"You should not have done that, Charlotte. They'll take away your business. Walt says you couldn't begin to put a Hercules down here. Anyway, we're fine. It's a lovely place. Interesting crevassing."

"I just couldn't bear it. I'm . . . I'm . . ."

"Charlotte, you must put that behind you. Do you understand? He would have wanted you . . ." The connection was lost.

They sat over their pure liquor in the sunshine. Their talk was mainly of aviation spirit. Walt had met this guy, at Mother Teresa's in Punta, who knew about a Russian drop, had the GPS, put in the Otters, come along for the ride, Johnny, we'll have fun. Johnny said that, at the Pole, Amundsen had two cans of paraffin, knew they wouldn't need them, they were just so fast on skis, those men, thought he should leave them for Scott and Bowers and Oates; but didn't, just in case; and dropped them on the Beardmore where Mr Swithinbank of the BAS found them in '78, intact, no creep, took the GPS, and left them, because of the Archaeology Protocol. But they killed Amundsen, they were with him, in the aeroplane that day when he took off from Bergen, flew into a cloud and was never seen again, like the great magician he was. Andy said, Was that in some book, so he could read it, at his own pace . . . And Johnny said, It's in the standard biography, my first wife gave it to me, I'll fax it to you, when I get home . . . And the word home made them fall back in the snow, what laughs they had, the Canadians and the British, among the roaring crevasses! And Walt said, For me, the greatest of them all was Shackleton, because when the *Endurance* broke up in the Weddell, you know the way the pressure ridges hit with the speed of a galloping horse, and all the men stood on the ice, ready to die, but he said, I'll bring you home, and he did, every single damn one of them, though he had to sail an open boat across eight hundred miles of ocean and walk across South Georgia to the Norwegians, such men . . . And Johnny said, Not just men, you know, look at Jane Franklin, sent ten boats through the ice to King William Island, just so her silly husband and his useless men should have a prayer said over them . . . And Andy said, What about that other British guy, Johnny Somebody, way back when, who took two ships into the Weddell and then . . . Oh Jesus. You amazing great Polish idiot, Padocki. It doesn't matter, Andy, Walt. He was a good navigator. And they made a song about him, which goes like this, and Johnny sang in Geordie to the continent:

With a hundred men from Moresbydale
From his Lady's bedside, Johnny did sail

and so on for nineteen verses, while Walt and Andy listened. They'd never heard a guy sing, just like that. Then he said: And if we come out of this, which I believe we will, you'll come over and land in a big field I have, though you must tell me in good time what you need by way of surface and length and wind-indication, and you can see my house and his portrait and hers, there's only one, she was very pretty, called Meg, worked in the cow yard, and his desk from the *Good Hope* and his charts and books and meet my wife.

Nor was Charlotte wholly idle in her office, with its tin roof and banks of lupins waving at the bright Magellan. Her first ports of call were senior officers of the Chilean and Argentine air forces – independently, mind – who kissed her hand and vowed, in the same language, to rescue the British lord and his brave aviators or die gloriously in the attempt;

and in these protestations, she sensed they had in mind, the one to emulate and the other to extinguish, the fame of Lt Luis Pardo who in April 1916 had taken a leaky tin tug named the *Yelcho*, which had never before been out of Punta roads, down into the ice and brought back Shackleton's men from Elephant Island. They became thoughtful when Charlotte pointed out, as honestly as she dared, that no fixed-wing aircraft might land at the glacier; and that the helicopter must be crated and taken with its crew and fuel by C-130 to Independence; and there despatched, with two halts to refuel at pre-dropped depots, the nine hundred nautical miles to Foundation Glacier; the whole to cost . . .well, Charlotte didn't estimate the cost.

The United States Navy did estimate the cost; and for a Sikorsky from Christchurch, New Zealand with its fixed-wing support, it was seven million dollars (a figure that included, I regret to say, a portion of the overhead of the Amundsen-Scott South Pole Base); and Charlotte must indemnify the Defense Department for the cost of the operation and surrender her commercial aviation licence. To these conditions, Charlotte readily assented. Unfortunately, Charlotte had no money: her aircraft were leased and her assets – aviation spirit cached under several feet of Antarctic snow and the various bent forks, Bakelite mugs, snow-shovels, insanitary saucepans, packets of Jell-o and the like at Independence Hills – were not, as they say, bankable: actually, no banker would lend her a red peso against them. Her rich clients in Beverly Hills and Jackson Hole and the South Tyrol were forever just stepping out of their offices when she called. It was inevitable, fair even, that Johnny should pay and, in truth, when Charlotte explained the situation in tears over the HF, he thought it a decent price for the lives of his new friends; but the Department now demanded his signature on the indemnity, which naturally was not possible. Charlotte telephoned Candida in Northumberland but, for some reason, she was not in and the housekeeper did not know her where-abouts. She overcame some scruple and telexed and then telephoned Downing Street, for Johnny had reminded her that Mrs Thatcher had an interest in the southern polar regions as the theatre of great feats of British arms and womanly leadership in 1982; but Charlotte proceeded no further than the Cabinet Secretary. Negotiations with the governments of New Zealand and India, and the President of the Disney company in Los Angeles, expired in legal and financial detail.

While Charlotte was incurring expenses in Latin America, there was at Independence Hills a trio of Norwegian military officers – whose leader, Torling Sporborg, now sits in the Storting – who had just completed some feat of sponsored skill and endurance and were making up their weight in the cook-shack. Over plastic plates piled mountainously with ten thousand kilo-calories apiece, in the endless sunshine, they began to whisper and, yes, it was theoretically possible: to dash the thirty days to the glacier, lightening their sleds as they went, pick up the starving maroons, and race back with them; and all for the thrill of the thing, and the glory of Norway, money, fame, the admiration of young women and the ghosts of Blaland and Captain Amundsen. The cost to Johnny this time would be a mere two million dollars, in recompense to their sponsors, for they would all have to overwinter at Independence.

Now Sporborg was a brilliant skier, and a brave young man, but he was no mathematician; and Johnny, who had picked up some things from his first wife and was, could not make the sums add up. For the Norwegians to start from Independence with food for three for thirty days and for six for thirty-five required sled loads of four hundred pounds each on the first day; with which weight not even Sporborg could ski the distance in thirty days, but in forty, nor return in thirty-five but in forty-five and so not four hundred pounds but four hundred and eighty pounds and so on round and round till Johnny's head ached and his eyes swam from the glare off the paper on which he did his calculations. The weather was getting worse. Every other day was lost to wind or white-out. The thermometer was dropping, by a degree a day. At times there was a hint of darkness in the sky and a fugitive flush of dawn. Even supposing the Norwegians could make the crossing, they would all set off back in darkness, running for their lives against starvation and the thermometer. Johnny was not deterred by the ordeal which, as Sporborg bragged by way of Charlotte in Punta, would truly be the Worst Journey in the World: Johnny had boundless admiration for the Norwegian school of Polar exploration. He had little doubt that Sporborg would eventually lope in to Independence in minus seventy-five degrees Fahrenheit, baying for fatback and Akvavit, but none of the others would and it seemed a bad bargain to sacrifice five lives instead of three. He rejected the plan and counterproposed that he and the pilots should hike off the glacier, a distance of some one hundred and twenty nautical miles, or about ten days since they had no skis, carrying fuel and trash with which to light a ski-way for the Navy Hercules. At that point, Walt said that instead of babying Charlotte over the High Frequency, Johnny might be better employed trying to find four hundred yards of usable surface right here before they starved. They'd exhausted the area round the aircraft, but had mapped and marked with canes a taxi-way to an area about three miles away, which looked to Johnny more promising.

Candida, too, was busy in her way. At a party in London that November, she was checking her coat when a man pushed past her towards the street door. He had on a pin-striped suit and a silk shirt open at the neck. He looked clean and independent like a cat. She glared at him and their eyes crossed. "Are you coming, Bellarmine?" he said, turned and pushed through the door. Candida retrieved her coat and ran up the pavement after him.

His name was Nicky de Soto. He traded derivatives, or bought and sold oil cargoes on the high seas, or financed leveraged takeovers. Whatever was fashionable on the edges of the financial markets – or rather just before it passed out of the *Financial Times* and into the *Daily Mail* – Nicky was doing it, as if to present a plausible livelihood. In reality, he gambled at the Valmont in Berkeley Square, a house he called his "office", as if aware of the brutal drudgery of his existence. His favoured game was backgammon and he was known to his acquaintanceship – truly or not, I don't know– as the best player in the country. That was his social predicate, though Candida preferred in introduction: Nicky plays backgammon. Otherwise, as far as she could tell, he had no house, father or mother, wife, child, bank account, age, nationality or place of birth, or any property but his suit and his black shoes and his cream silk shirts.

Why did Candida like him, and so much that she spent that autumn in London? Not for his love-making, for in bed he was frigid; nor, I'm sure, for his unkindness. I think she liked the society he provided her, the celebrities he knew and who knew him. When she stood with Nicky at these treadmill entertainments, not too close, she was excited by a knowing flicker in these people's glances: that, by cheating on her husband, she'd entered some hyper-reality of fashion. "How's Johnny?" they said, for he was still a rich lord. "At the South Pole," she said, and the answer satisfied everybody. She liked Nicky's splendid rudeness to nonentities. As they were whipped and scourged from party to party, Candida sensed she was at the heart of modernity and that something marvellous – history, maybe– was being made. In the early hours, she was moved to tears by the elegance of her new friends.

What she loved, I believe, was money. For in November and December of 1986, Candida discovered money. Cascades of money passed over her and through her hands and down her back. She found it possible, and then necessary, to spend ten thousand pounds on a dress. And in these beautiful clothes – by Abderrahime and Smitty – she felt sheathed not in leather and lace but in money at its most diaphanous. Perhaps she spent to see how much she had. If so, she did not find out. Battersby wrote often and she signed papers and moved accounts from there to here.

Nicky let her pay for things. For him, money had but one form and that precious: banknotes, which he carried on him. He also let her extinguish one debt, a margin call on some sugar in Chicago, of eighty thousand dollars: which, no doubt, was quite wrong of her, but it was nothing to what her husband was attempting to spend.

On Christmas Eve, Nicky said: "You can come to Ste-Berthe, but you'll have to pay your way and look after yourself." Candida didn't care. Delivered from the piety and folklore of the Wexley Park Christmas, she ate caviar with the Esterhazy-Blacks and skinny-dipped with Gina Cambazolos. Nicky, who was restless anywhere after an hour, left for a tournament in Las Vegas, Nevada; but Candida stayed and saw in her friends' smiles a tremor of approval. She had done her eating as a Turpe; and spun her Bellarmine pupa; and now emerged, gorgeous, aerial and free. Around her all was order and beauty, luxury, calm and delight. She went to Acapulco with the Grunfelds, then Aspen, then Palm Beach, and then New York.

It was in New York that men started asking her about the pheasants at Wexley Park and the spring salmon in the More. She realised she missed her husband, not just as a woman misses a man with whom she shares a bed, but because he was her husband: she still believed she needed such an appendage. When she telephoned Wexley Park to learn he had still not returned from his holiday, she was angry as never before; because she was frightened for her future.

Often, as he worked, Johnny would become aware of somebody beside him: not a human being necessarily, but animate and vivid and sad. He'd look up from the snow, gaze about him, see Walt leaning on his ski-pole, or Andy seated on the snow with his legs apart, and the rope that joined them snaking over the sastrugi, and the snow and the crevasses and the tail of the Otter in the distance. He'd shake his head, and go back to prodding, sometimes teetering on his boot-heels, as a snow-bridge collapsed, or tumbling on to the shock of the rope in his armpits. Something had gone liquid in his mind. He supposed that death casts its shadow over a person's last days, and that's why he had such trouble beating Walt and Andy out of their bags, and why he himself was caring less. And all the while he sensed about him a third presence.

"Jane?"

"Yes, Johnny."

He didn't look up.

"What am I to do?"

"Why not tell me what you're doing."

Johnny sighed. "We need four hundred yards of surface . . ."

"Have you lightened the aeroplane?"

"Yes, Jane. I've taken out the spare tanks, rations, personal bags, all seats but Walt's, cabin insulation, cabin heater, High Frequency radio . . ."

"What about the wheels? They're worth a minimum of twenty-five yards."

"We need them. To land on the mainland . . ."

"I think that's thinking rather far ahead, isn't it, my darling? I thought the matter was to get out of here . . ."

He stole a glance. She was wearing a blue down jacket, grey wind-proof trousers, ski-boots, a Russian hat and sun-glasses. She had a bad sunburn on both cheeks.

"Jane, it's no good. I can't even find ninety yards in a straight line."

"So you'll have to take off on the bias."

"What do you mean, Jane? You're not making sense. We won't have the power to . . ."

"You will if you bank the curve."

"Oh," said Johnny.

"Are you starving, Johnny?"

"I don't know. Probably. You see, I put us on five hundred calories a day. I thought . . ."

She looked down and made a mark with her boot-toe in the snow. "I don't think that's a good idea, Johnny. Surely somebody can arrange a drop of food, can't they?"

"They did. The Chileans sent a DC-9. It had to turn back over the Peninsula, crash-landed at King George Island." He looked at her shyly. "They're not best pleased with me."

Jane sighed. She said: "You're not going to survive the winter whatever happens. You must go back up to two thousand calories. You need your strength. To build the banks, I mean."

"Yes, Jane."

"And Johnny, you're going to have to do it." Her eyes passed over his shoulder. "I don't think your friends are . . ."

"I know, Jane."

"Do you need me to calculate the speed and slope for you? For the neutral steer, I mean."

Johnny shook his head. "It's all right. Thank you, Jane."

"Don't thank me! I'm a figment of your imagination. Thank God, if you must."

"I don't believe in God."

"Now he tells us!"

For a minute, Johnny stood still, looking into the distance. Then he walked to the Otter, and returned after a while with a snow shovel and a calculator and two Hershey bars.

While the pilots slept, Johnny went for a walk. He took a ski-pole, a VHF radio and the cockpit instrument Andy called the Magellan or the GPS; which stands, I believe, for Global Positioning System while Magellan Corp., of Santa Monica, California, is a well-known United States manufacturer of such instruments.

He went slowly, at first, wishing he'd once in his life learned to ski; but found, after a while, that in the horizontal midnight sunshine he could see a faint shadow on the snow which indicated crevasses. He walked, with many detours, for about eight hours, not thinking about much, or indeed anything. The tail of Kilo Bravo disappeared over the curve of the earth, but the incandescent mountains came no nearer. He stopped, I suppose because he was tired, and looked at the mountains of the Dufek Range and, through them, at eternity: a place that was cold and dry and bright and beautiful past mortal toleration, not sad or busy, but beyond affection and event. He saw that all his life to that moment had been provisional, that everything had been or was becoming something else, but no longer. He said: Blast. Then, he put down his ski-pole and knelt for a time in the snow.

Then he took out the GPS, and, taking off his gloves, sent a signal: which, careering between three satellites roaming the clean stratosphere, returned to him in three pieces of information in red LED: latitude, longitude and altitude. The first two he wrote down in the book he was carrying. As to altitude, he knew he was high up, that he'd walked on buried Everests.

On the way back, he tried to urinate beside his outgoing track and saw that he was dehydrated, to death. He did the last part on his face.

Fortunately, the white gas stove was lit and, though he didn't have the strength to lift a shovel, he put in snow in handfuls, and, when it melted, poured it down his throat from his goggles. In the cabin of the Otter, over the thunder of the pilots' snores, he drank eleven sachets of strawberry Kool-Aid and, smiling a little, wrote a letter: which, carried in the pocket of his down jacket for three weeks (while Walt took the Otter singing into the rose twilight and by slow, dark, blind, freezing stages up the Peninsula and over the Drake to a hard landing at Punta Arenas, Chile) and posted from a whorehouse in that town known as Mama Teresa's, where Johnny had invited them to dance, Charlotte and the pilots – the Norwegians having been overcome by shyness at the street door – just to dance, mind, they were all married guys – though all night and half-way to noon– and the girl called Concepcion kissed his frost-bit nose and cheeks and Andy lurched, menacing, on to the pitching dance-floor, roaring in Calgary Spanish – and Charlotte said, crying with happiness, This girl has also got to go to work! – ; which letter arrived, grubby with distance and time and happiness, on the astonished desk of the senior partner of Purlingbrook in Lincoln's Inn; and that gentleman, after making some adjustments to diminish its elegance and clarity, and commissioning and notarising a Spanish translation, consigned it to his dreary safe; though safes have never bothered me. The letter read, after a conventional opening:

That, being of sound Mind and Body, and weary of this World of Appearances but in no Wise presuming to delay or hasten its Abridgement, do instruct

That, in conformity with the Spirit and Letter of the Antarctic Treaty (1959), and all Amendments and Protocols entered into by the signatory Nations either prior or subsequent to this Instrument; and the Laws of the United Kingdom and the Republics of Chile and Argentina; and of all Agreements and Understandings between these Powers, pending a Resolution of all Claims of Sovereignty and Jurisdiction as they relate to the Territory mentioned hereinunder; and of all Laws and

Regulations as they relate to Civil Aviation in the Territories known for the purposes of the Antarctic Treaty (1959), and all Amendments and Protocols thereto, as the Antarctic Continent, including the Place mentioned hereinunder and the Air-Space above it; such Regulations to include those of the United Kingdom Civil Aviation Authority and the United States Federal Aviation Adminstration and the Air Traffic Control Inspectorate of the Republic of Chile and the Armed Forces Aeronautics Directorate of the Republic of Argentina

That, at my death, my body be taken to the Place known as Foundation Glacier, and there, at a Latitude of 83° 47' South and a Longitude of 113° 05' West, be laid upon the Snow, where it shall be shrouded in an Instant; and in the aeons of Antarctic glacial Time, be crushed by accumulating Ice until it is Nothing

And that the Aviators, who carry my Body to said Place, shall be well rewarded for their Skill and Courage, at the Discretion of my sole Executor

And that, if, at the Liquidation of my Estate, after all Payments of Pension and Annuity, and the Conversion of my Tenancies in Favour of their Incumbents into Holdings in Fee simple, *gratis*, all Costs to be borne by the Estate; and the Satisfaction of all reasonable Creditors, secured and unsecured; if, these Conditions being satisfied, there be not sufficient Monies in the Estate to reward the said Air-Men or -Women, that these Monies be raised from public Subscription, at the Discretion of my sole Executor

And that, should any Property remain to my Estate, after the Satisfaction of these Consignments, that it be sold and the Proceeds distributed, at the Discretion of my sole Executor whom I hereby name as Jane, Countess of Bellarmine and Rokeby and Viscountess Antrim, to the Homeless and Destitute of the City of Newcastle

And that the said Jane, Countess Bellarmine, do say a
Prayer to God Almighty
for my worthless Soul.

Jane and Charlotte met in 1987, at the Women Mean Business Award,
sponsored by the *Evening Standard* at the Dorchester Hotel. Jane,
who was somewhat expert in these events, announced the winners and
handed out the statuettes. She found the food inedible.

At some stage in the interminable banquet, Charlotte said:

"I flew Johnny south last season."

"Lucky old you."

The table quivered with pleasure and alarm. A fight, a fight! Two
women, Scotch, pretty, and hard as nails, the both!

Charlotte said: "I wasn't boasting, Jane. I was apologising."

Jane looked at her. She thought: Strange, isn't it, when you lose your
love, how your mind goes blizzardy like a snowstorm, don't you find,
you lose your judgement. She leaned over and kissed the other woman
on the face; which the table found also kind of nice, in its way.

But poor Candida had no such succour in her blizzard, from Jane or
anybody. She hated his beard and the marks on his face, and crying in
his sleep or sitting bolt upright in bed, shivering, his skin icy-cold, and
the bloody woman calling from South America at all hours, what's he
been up to down there, the cheat, and the stupefying lectures at the
RGS and those awful Canadians who landed in the Slings and called
her Lady and wore their caps indoors and jeans at dinner . . . and . . .
and. She spent quite a lot of time at a flat near Sloane Square.

Meanwhile, Johnny made some alterations to his investments.
He travelled to Lime Street in London and there put his affairs into
the hands of God, or rather of the instrument of His will in that part
of London, Mr R.W. Turpe.

10

Of the masterpieces of literature that have insurance for their subject, I am familiar only with *Rob Roy*, which was written by Sir Walter Scott in 1817 and deals with events in Scotland a hundred years before. In truth, the insurance Rob sold was primitive even for that epoch: for it covered only depredation by Rob Roy MacGregor and his gillies. "A very singular contract of assurance," say the scandalised merchants of the novel; and yet it is Rob who saves them from bankruptcy. It is as if Scott believed that old-fashioned aristocratic honour and modern commercial credit were complementary; or perhaps he was homesick for an era when the division of labour was less rigid and economists moonlighted as footpads.

Of Roderick Wynyates Turpe what would Scott have said? Would he have cast him as an antique hero adrift in commercial modernity? Should snobbery, the regimental style of doing business and the resentments of small boarding schools be my plaid, dirk and claymore: elements of a rich and disordered past to be cherished in fiction now they can do no harm? Is there tragedy in Roddie's story and the social class he brought to grief?

Roddie was guilty of several technical business offences with which I shall not trouble you. His moral fault, and Cecilia's – the fault that allowed the other faults in – was that they had no interest in commerce, merely in riches; and in that they differed from all the other characters in this story. And these riches they did not convert to use, to educate themselves like Stephen and Johnny, but to embed themselves in that most transient of realities: society. Henry Adams, an American who lived in London in the 1860s, discovered something important about England which his friend Henry James made the theme of a great novel called *The Wings of the Dove*. It is that in England (less Scotland) money is always aspiring to the condition of real estate. In other words, the spoils of commerce, piracy or venal matrimony have no social reality until converted into things. Money, in short, must be laundered.

The money Roddie siphoned away from Lime Street, scooped out with his pitcher from the flood of money coursing down that thoroughfare, was translated by Cecilia into property – two pairs of Purdy shotguns, a cottage near Newmarket, some Old Master drawings, a week's fishing on the Helmsdale river in Sutherland, a done-up farmhouse near Siena – which then whispered this message to the world: This is us, like the Bellarmines, but less stuffy and more fun. And this social project had for its aim not to secure positions for their son and daughter, who anyway had other fish to fry; but to reverse or abolish their own social past. Roddie's father had been discharged only a Major in a Signals regiment which, for some reason I don't understand, was a bad thing. Cecilia's mother had been divorced by a banker and for some time kept a decorator's shop on the Caribbean island of St Lucia, which ditto.

The society they craved was in the opposite condition. Its wealth was not in money but in property, and yet it needed money to feed; and rather than sell its houses and farms and pictures and ponies for money, it wanted to enjoy their comfort and social amenity and yet also have money. For it was as if these people held their property in mortmain, motionless and inalienable; and they themselves were the perfect and eternal culmination of uncountable sequences of social evolution. Yet within their houses and fields, they sensed there was something hidden, which was not beauty or utility or some other value, but a representative of all values: they scented money as horses scent water. Farms, woods, barns, pictures, animals, securities: Roddie carted them off to Lime Street not in body but in essence, as the phantom capital of his insurance ventures; and the squire or lady, rising each morning to see the Ferneley in its wonted place above the sideboard in the dining room, and the sideboard itself, forgot those objects were at risk of fire or shipwreck ten thousand miles away; forgot, indeed, that they no longer owned them. For money, which is perfectly mobile and utterly indifferent, is a terrible destroyer of social form.

In Chapter One, I showed you the Turpes working the drawing room at Wexley Park. I might just as easily have taken you outdoors and shown you the Roddie of the open air, striding over the heather, a sun-burned figure in salmon-pink socks; or mincing towards you across the saturated plough, an emerald fox glinting in his tie; or curvetting past you in Bembridge bay or roll-casting upstream of you in the endless Naver twilight or scooping a one-under from the eighteenth at the Belfry or cracking with touts on Lambourn Downs. R.W. Turpe! Was ever worldly ruin so plausibly impersonated? How could you have known that at that moment – moor, plough, river – when you heard him say, Shared, I think, old boy; or lost hounds, old man; or broke me in the Potts, the swine– that it were better that you had never been born. A class in decline meets a class on the make; they combine; and detonate.

Of all the Members Agents at Lloyd's at this period, Roddie was the stupidest; and if I have contrasted him with Jane, it is not from gallantry but economics: the first woman will be very much wiser and better than the last man. Yet Roddie could see that business was going to hell; and though I don't think he ever formed the thought, I'd last five seconds against Ira Rothenstein – for he was addicted to an Edwardian attitude to Jews in business – he knew he was not equal to the Alaska claim. I think sometimes after dinner, mute with port, he saw the problem of Old Years as more than just unfunded liabilities from dusty insurance policies in the morgues of United States corporations; and understood that there is no such thing as insurance on the earth; that human activity leaves injuries that cannot be redeemed by money; that there is more to history than probability and compound interest; and that when the oil company Shell, between the years of 1953 and 1968, at a place near Denver, Colorado, called the Rocky Mountain Arsenal, burned chemical waste in open drums in pits which were then merely back-filled, the injury was not just to the Herefords that died in thousands at polluted water-holes, the hecatombs of sandhill cranes and tufted ducks, or even to the company's re-insurers at Lloyd's, about thirty thousand families of the English and Scots gentry; but to the people of the United States, and their descendants, and the land, and even, who knows, God in his great patience; for the place was, in the words of Capt. Donnelly, of the US Army Corps of Engineers in his report of 1968, "putrefied for eternity". So that when the catastrophes began to fall like hail on the standing crops of Lime Street – not just the English storm you know about, or the *Zenon Bellarmine*, but the catastrophes of 1988 and 1989, the explosion on an oil platform in the North Sea named Piper Alpha, a hurricane among the sprouting sub-divisions of Southern Florida, another storm in Western Europe, a fire among the movie mansions of Malibu – these seemed truly to be Acts of God.

But Roddie and Cecilia hadn't the metaphysics to contemplate these signs; and since Roddie was a cheery sort of chap, and the 1987 profit and loss wouldn't be published for three years – for that was Lloyd's practice, to allow the bulk of the claims to come in – he felt something would turn up. So he would not return Stephen's calls, poncy little yid, or reply to the letter he received from Stephen and Jane; and when it was published in the *Financial Times*, more or less in full with a leader and a witty tail-note in the *Lex* column, he made Jock Marshall's life a misery and roared down the phone at the young men and women of the *Lex* column, whose intelligence greatly exceeded their experience of society. To reporters, he fulminated against Brimberg's, and, off the record, questioned Jacob Brimberg's motives; and though that firm had nothing but contempt for Turpe and Lloyd's, and indeed for everything not bounded by the quadrilateral made by Lombard Street, Cornhill, Princes Street and London Wall, Stephen came before the Management Committee and passed what the French call *un mauvais quart d'heure*. Jacob thought Jane overrated – his wives were blonde – and though he cared not at all who succeeded him at the firm, he wanted there to be more than one candidate. Stephen was not sorry when Jane rang to ask if perhaps he was intending to go to Alaska.

For our heroine, Turpe reserved a special humiliation. He called a press conference at Lime Street for his toy reporters – the *FT* was disinvited – and, over the bloody marys, flourished a record of her visit to Lime Street and her clearly expressed interest in investing in the LMX market. On deep background, and more in sorrow than in anger, he gave some information on the alliance of marriage of the Turpes and Bellarmines. It was no use Jane, from Burlington Street, telling the reporters that it was only in the process of investigation that she had come to her conclusions, which she stood by in her private capacity; and she had no hard feelings towards her ex-husband and his wife. The reporters made hay with her embarrassment. The person they had created – that paragon of manufacturing and femininity! – now bored them. It was time to knock her down, as a child kicks down an afternoon's sandcastle.

Such is the nature of publicity. But Turpe had made a great error. For in refusing to tackle a problem as it arose – the essence of business management – he set an example to the Names at Lloyd's which was to bring the entire market to grief. For when, three years later, the horror of their ruin at last penetrated their innocence, they shrieked and rebelled and pulled the Lime Street temple crashing about their ears. But that lies beyond our story. Let me just say this: once, in the winter of 1993, hurrying down Princes Street in rain beneath the long wall of the Bank of England, I passed a man in a stove-pipe hat and cape, bent into the wind, and turning saw it was great Nathan, weeping for his commercial heirs.

But we must return to real time, 15 November, 1987, on which day Jane's life took a turn for the worse.

So small was the circulation of *Workers Week*, and smaller still its readership, and so dense the dialectical style of Tom Sale, that it was a week before the other newspapers had heard of Cathy McKay; and even though the components of the story were all embedded there – Jane, Cathy, the QE Works, the prostitute, the Piggeries – it was so encrusted in analysis – for to Tom, individual morality merely reflected class morality – that the busy tabloid journalists had some trouble reconstructing the story in bourgeois language. Jane first heard of Cathy and the death agonies of capitalism, opening the door of her flat at the Bagatelle early on that Sunday morning.

The reporter, a man, very nervous, garbled his question: "So who's your sister?"

Still dazed with sleep, Jane said: "I haven't got a sister."

The reporter turned away and then, remembering himself, said:

"But you are Judy McKay's daughter, aren't you?" He smiled reassuringly.

"May I see that?"

"Sure."

Jane, now awake, took the *Sunday People* and closed the door and didn't open it again all that day. She started reading the article, but it made no sense to her: it was as if her life had been demolished, and rebuilt in some cheap and anachronistic material. Much was attributed to friends, of whose existence she had not until then been aware but would have welcomed. When the telephone rang, she disconnected it. By inserting the phone jack, and then immediately breaking the line, she managed to make some calls herself: first, to a food manufacturing company in Bradenton, Iowa, where there was no answer; to international directory enquiries; to the Holiday Inn in that pleasant little farm town, where she heard that Mr Cohen and Ms Madden had checked out already; to directory assistance again; and to a subscriber in South America.

"*¿Se puede hablar con Señora Meredith?*"

"Jane! It's so lovely to hear your voice again. Let me turn this bloody thing off."

"Charlotte, I wonder if you could possibly do me a favour. You see . . . Charlotte, are you there?"

"I'm listening, Jane."

"You see, I have a business problem, rather a serious one. Also I'm quite unhappy, and for some reason don't seem to have any friends.

I wonder if you could bear to come to London to be with me, just for a bit, I'll pay of course . . ."

"Jane, I can't. It breaks my heart. I've got thirty-six dentists coming in from Santiago, and eight of them have lost their gear; and a new airplane; and I need six thousand gallons of fuel and haven't got cash or credit . . ."

"For God's sake," said Jane. "Who are your bankers? Would ten thousand dollars cover it?"

"I can't, Jane. It's *Banco Nacional de Chile* in Punta, there's only one branch. Could you make it fifteen? Look, darling, what I'll do is get the Hercules off my back and meet you in New York next weekend. I'll ask Sagacedad to get us rooms at the Carlyle. We'll lie around in our underwear, eating chocolates and drinking Jack Daniel's and smoking dope and watching dirty movies on cable . . ."

"You slept with him, didn't you, you bitch."

"Jane, you may not speak to me like that. Do you hear? Pull yourself together. Whoever told you life was easy? Well, it ain't. You just have to go on."

"I'm sorry, Charlotte. Please forgive me. It's just . . ."

"You sound like you're ready for a trip south. Please, Jane, come in with us. I mean it. It would make such a difference to have somebody with your reputation. Every time that fucking aircraft takes off, I just stand on the tarmac, wanting to die. Something awful is just waiting to happen. The US Navy wants to close me down. The Chileans are just using us, because they're too smart to fly. Hugo would just be so tickled to know from up there you're chairman, instead of that dopey General . . ."

"I know nothing of aviation."

"So who does?"

"Steve Cohen's in the US," Jane said wearily. "Maybe he could come down and do a valuation, if you're serious."

"I've got no profits, Jane."

"You have assets."

"I haven't! I've got fuel with a cost value of eight hundred thousand dollars pre-positioned in Antarctica, but because it has to be taken out again under the Treaty, it's not an asset but a massive liability. I have an incredible negative net worth. Girls always do. That's why I can't borrow."

"Fascinating," said Jane. "But you have a monopoly."

"I have a monopoly."

"Let me get this clear, Charlotte. You have a monopoly of commercial aviation in Antarctica?"

"Yes, Jane."

"And the third-party exposure?"

"We're OK under Chilean law because of the waiver they sign."

"What about outside Chilean jurisdiction?"

"It's Antarctica, sweetest."

"I see. What about half a million for fifty-one per cent?"

"Forty-nine per cent."

"All right."

"But you must be involved. Chairman or at the fucking least executive director. The board meets monthly in New York."

"All right," Jane said. "Who's your lawyer?"

"Mort Spielman at Millbank Tweed."

"Well, they can sort it out. Thank you, Charlotte, you've saved my life."

"Any time, darling. Oh and Jane . . ."

"I'll wire the fifteen thousand first thing tomorrow . . ."

"Do that. What I wanted to say was: I didn't. Though not for want of trying."

"I don't mind, Charlotte."

"Please go to sleep, Jane. Do you want me to stay on the line?"

"I'm fine. Goodbye, Charlotte."

"Goodbye."

The next morning, a Monday, Jane took especial care with her clothes and hair. As she descended into the lobby, the porter lost himself in an electrical task.

Jane's appearance, through the swing-doors of the Bagatelle, wearing a lipstick and in a dark suit and carrying papers, caught the reporters off balance and she was half-way up Arlington Street before they could lumber up to her in their Barbour jackets. At first she let the questions fly at her, praying that nobody would actually touch her; but the questions came in through her ears and must have appeared in her face as utter perplexity; for the reporters became milder.

Somebody said: "We're just doing our job, Jane. There's a genuine public interest."

And Jane, sensing an opportunity, stopped dead, and looking at her feet, said: "When I know a bit more, I'll call you to Burlington Street, I promise, and answer every question I can."

With that, she strode towards Piccadilly and the reporters fell away, for they had some scruple. Not so the photographers and camera-people, for their job was to record the face of human sorrow; and they pressed in close with their Canons and video-cameras, and because Jane continued to stare straight ahead of her, shouted things at her, to make her turn in fear and rage to the lens.

"Hey, here, fat-tits."

"Here, bitch, here."

This worked admirably; and the pictures of Jane that appeared on television, and in the morning editions, in their madness and misery, seemed merely to confirm the story's public interest. During this crucifixion-walk, round by the Ritz and along its colonnade, the wide pavement allowing easy circulation for the photographers, waiting for the pedestrian light to turn green, Jane also thought: I am a child to have such an obsessional routine. Henceforth, I will travel only behind dark glass, a different route every day. At Green Park tube, she was left alone. Perhaps the men had enough still film and videotape of her; perhaps the light in the booking-hall was too poor for them to work by; and perhaps, most likely, the plebeian transportation unsettled these professionals.

At Burlington Street, there was another cohort, but here Jane had the assistance of Pete, who was not too delicate to stand on toes and sky video-cameras, accidentally, with his shoulder. Upstairs, he took her coat, set her at her desk, and gave her a plastic cup of rum. On the telephone, he was fluent: "I'm afraid Mrs Haddon has just stepped out. May I say who's calling?" Averting his eyes, he selected one of the telephone slips and, when Jane came to stand by him again, passed it across to her. Jane didn't look at it. She thought: It's important, I think, not to show a weakness, especially what's thought of as feminine weakness, such as bursting into tears, going to the ladies etc.

Pete said over a covered mouthpiece: "The shares are at sixty-three pence, Jane."

"Pete, did you ever come across an outfit called the Workers Party at acting school?"

Pete earthed the phone. "Yes."

"Do you happen to know where they are?"

"Somewhere in South London. Clapham High Street? No, Streatham High Street. Or were. I can find out."

"Would you do that for me?"

All the while, Joe Morris was standing in his door; and the experience of his morning, the radio news, the newspapers, the mob at the door, and now these Bolsheviks, made him feel he should have taken that partnership from Price Waterhouse. He turned, but Jane called after him:

"How much cash have we, Joe?"

Definitely taken it. "I don't know exactly."

"You don't know, Joe. Well, I imagine we have between forty and forty-five million pounds in cash and cash equivalents. What are you going to do with this forty to forty-five million pounds in cash and near-cash? You are going, please, to call Jacob Brimberg and say we are buyers up to sixty-seven . . ."

"You can't do that, Jane!"

"Why not, Joe?"

"You haven't the authority."

"I most certainly do have the authority, from the last annual general meeting, to purchase up to ten per cent of the ordinary shares which is a great deal more than forty-five million even at sixty-seven pence a share. Please just do as I ask."

"But it's working capital. We need every cent . . ."

Jane shivered in exasperation. She said: "The shares of Associated British Textiles have fallen by a third in the first half-hour of trading this morning. The stock market believes I will be fired. In that, it may be right. But it is quite wrong in supposing I am worth three hundred million pounds to this company. I am not worth a penny a share. This difference in valuation presents a business opportunity."

At length, Joe said: "You'll have to inform the Stock Exchange."

"Would you also do that for me?"

Joe turned and closed the door to his office and so missed things far more disturbing to his peace of mind: Pete hugging his chest with both arms and saying:

"I'll handle all the calls till twelve. But between twelve and one I have an appointment, which I can't cancel. So you don't answer the phone at all, Jane, do you understand?"

"Oh Pete, I promised to come with you. I'm coming."

"They'll eat you up outside. We're all alone, Jane."

"No you're not."

Turning to her office, she tried to think of other consolation, and lit on a phrase of her late mother-in-law's. She said: "Whichever way it goes, try to remember who you are, Pete."

"I'll try," he said, and began to shake.

Jane wired the dollars to Chile and spoke three times on the telephone that morning. The first time was at nine-thirty.

Over the intercom, Pete said: "Meg Tomkins?" Pete was, as he had realised some time ago with a shrug, a better secretary than actor.

"Thank you, Pete."

"Jane?" The voice was distant, inexperienced: as if to Meg, the telephone were something atrocious, to be used only in emergencies.

"Oh Meg, it's so nice to hear from you."

"We were thinking, Jane . . ." She corrected herself, way out there in Dovedale. "Bill was thinking perhaps you'd like to come to us for a few days. Till this awful thing blows over." Whenever Johnny's sister had an unconventional thought, she liked to attribute it to her husband. This good man, Reader in and perhaps one day Professor of Philosophy at Sheffield University, had been surprised, then touched, then irritated, then pleased by this habit of his wife's.

"Meg, I don't think it would be . . ."

"What do you mean, Jane? I don't understand you."

Ah, thought Jane, it cost her something, this. You're so damn stupid, Janet.

"What are you saying, Jane?" Margaret Tomkins, née Bellarmine, was cross.

"You're so kind, Meg, both of you. It's just I can't really think straight at the moment. But may I call you, if things really get horrible? I'm so grateful to you, Meg."

"Of course you can. That's what I was saying." Out there in the Peak, in her apron, a child squeezing each of her thighs and shrieking at her, Meg unbent a little. "Lots of love," she said, and replaced the potent instrument.

Then at eleven o'clock:

"Yes, it's Jane Haddon. May I speak to the minister?"

"Mrs Haddon, it's the Secretary of State now."

"No. I mean the minister, Mr Burke."

"He's Secretary of State, as I've been trying to tell you. It'll be on the twelve o'clock news. And at Agriculture!"

Jane wept.

The third conversation she had at noon.

Pete on the intercom again at five to twelve: "Connie for Himself, Jane."

"Please hold her a moment."

She left her office, took her secretary by the hand, smoothed down his hair, straightened his black Armani suit. Then they left the room by different doors, into their own ordeals.

"James, it's Jane."

"What the fuck do you think you're doing? Why the fuck didn't you return my call? Fucking Nixon's been on."

"I've been a little busy, James."

Jane had suspected all along, that if things turned mean, neither businessman was to be trusted.

"Well, you're not going to be from now on."

"James, at the time of the demerger, you said that I was a good manager, by far the best person you had and that I could have Textiles for five years without interference . . ."

"That didn't mean a bloody strike and drugs and some bloody family story . . ."

"Please let me finish, James. Those five years are not up and our agreement holds. In just three years, I have substantially deleveraged the business, moved from loss into profit, and paid dividends increasing at a rate twice that of general inflation. I also told you that I had taken drugs."

"Shit, Jane, I thought it was pot or coke, like Taki."

"You didn't enquire further."

Sweet Lord Doncaster, please fire me. Didn't work out. Mutual agreement. Board grateful for her service. Spend more time with her family. Not family. Pursue other interests.

"You're fired, Jane. Get yourself a lawyer. I'll be generous."

"And who, James Doncaster, is going to preserve your tin-horn little business empire when you're in the rest-home?"

There was silence and the Atlantic. Both were stunned into silence. She heard traffic, an ambulance racing towards Lenox Hill, and his breathing. She thought: Only joking, Jimmy. Let me go. Please let me go.

Lord Doncaster said: "I want to know, and I want to know now, what you are going to do."

"I am working with Hartmann on a joint venture, which will finance the new line without a pay cut, and also improve the terms of the Employee Stock-Ownership Plan. I bought the stock for distribution to employees this morning at a substantial discount to net-asset value and on a price/earnings ratio of four and a half. The employees will now have full and immediate dividend rights without any dilution to existing shareholders. If the employees do not accept the improved terms and break their contracts by going on strike, I will lock them out, pay off suppliers, dismantle the plant and sell it, probably, to a trade buyer. I have expressions of interest from businesses in Taipei in the Republic of China and Bangalore in South India. Then I will sell the land."

"I don't believe you, Jane. You have some crazy attachment to that place."

Too damn right I do, m'lord.

"You have a week."

Lord Doncaster put the phone down at his end, took off his bow-tie and dinner jacket, and actually had a thought for once. It was: When you came in to Cenci that evening, in your ridiculous bloody dress-for-success suit and trainers, quoting from professors nobody had heard of, and not eating for nerves, I must have known that you were Death; or rather, as I as author should interject, whatever Elysium is set aside by God for the ash of CEOs.

Jane thought: I will continue in business, but in a somewhat different way. I will ride to work and back again in a long car with dark windows like that fool James Doncaster, and they'll say: What style!. I will pay myself one and a quarter million pounds a year, with a further three and a half million in stock options. I will not invest in the factories to match their depreciation, but milk them and eventually dismantle them; and once Textiles is a bloated shell of cash, I will use it to terrorise every vulnerable company in the stock market, so that just a hint to the Sunday papers or an announcement to the London stock exchange that Mrs Haddon has bought fourteen point five per cent of the shares of Amalgamated Misery and is seeking a meeting with its directors will be enough to send its stock through the roof and drench me with capital gains; and I'll work from the Bagatelle, with just Pete and a cook, and accept no invitations and read only the third- and second-to-last pages of the *Financial Times* and take calls only from the senior partner of Cazenove; so that everybody says, Do you know she lives off morphine and chocolate and vintage port, never goes out, gets more than the Civil List and gives to cats' homes, and doesn't use her title, there should be a law against people like her.

Jane sighed. It would have to be New York. England was too small and silly. She'd buy that little house on 11th Street, even if it cost ten millions and a woman came to the door in a wimple, carrying a candle and grumbling in Dutch, and live by night, with Pete and a cook, and take calls only from Michael, and only when it suited her; till men in Akron, Ohio and Kalamazoo, Michigan held rallies against her in corporate parking lots, wearing Stop Jane! badges on the lapels of their Sears suits and the whole continent came to hate and fear her as much as silly England, and threw her into Leavenworth for seven years on some forged SEC complaint.

But of all the possible futures for Jane, that one I rejected, not because it arose in the disturbed part of her nature, or because it was implausible, because it wasn't, but because she still had a single tie to the old world. And, at that moment, she was jerked from her self-hatred by that tie; by Pete falling into the room in a hurricane of tears, and dropping her cigarette, she ran and caught him, though his weight felled her to the carpet; for Jane, like many people in business and politics, fancied her secretary.

And as he lay sprawled in her lap, sucking and sobbing tears on her lap, she felt his manliness, and also his diversion of it away from her, but curiously not the virus that would kill him, as sure as night follows day. Yet she said what she had long ago prepared for saying: "You are going to make the best of it, Pete. We should all treat each day as if it were our last. You can live your life in this time more intensely than most people do in three score and ten. And I'll be with you all the time, I promise you."

Pete shook in her lap, but from his multiple convulsions, she could not know he was shaking his head. But she saw Joe Morris' door open at the noise, and him gape at them over his white shirt, not in sympathy at a woman comforting a man condemned to death, but at his horribly splayed legs, her disordered hair, her cheeks wet with tears, her torn blouse showing an R & S bra and much else besides, and the fag burning the carpet square, and he turned in terror; slammed the door;

and because the windows weren't the sort that opened, Jane being stingy in matters of office accommodation as in all else, took the only way out, which was the telephone: precisely to the senior partner's secretary at the accounting firm of Price Waterhouse, saying that, after all, he had changed his mind, and would be happy to accept a partnership, if it was still on offer.

But Jane's instincts were, as usual, correct. For, in this mess of tears and misery, she finally disentangled a word, which was Negative. Pete was crying for another reason. I think he wept rather as my mother's father must have wept when a staff officer jerked him out of the line an hour before the maroon on the first day of the Somme. I mean, Pete wept not because the coolies had arrived at Boulogne and he was the only man in France that day who could speak Hankow Chinese worth a damn, and get the Chinks off the tramp and to work – actually, people who know said my grandfather spoke it marvellously, better than any Englishman, or rather Ulsterman; and, but for those Chinese, staring indifferently at the Boulogne mole from the decks, there'd be no me and no Jane and no Pete; God save the great people of China!; but that's all by the way – both men wept as they ran back in safety, one from the salient at Beauforêt and the other from the Soho Clinic, because they felt, in their incandescent joy and relief, such sadness that you and I, I hope, will never feel; that their generation was going into the wire; and that they were not.

Jane tried to lift him up. He rose, first into a stoop, and then into her chair.

"Well, shall we try and keep it that way, Pete?"

Pete looked terrified. "Your breast is showing, Jane."

Jane made some adjustments to her dress and stamped on the smouldering carpet.

She said: "Shall we get back to work? I want you to go to accountancy night school. The company will pay. This is for two reasons. The first is that it will keep you out of trouble in the evening till you've got your mind round this thing, dear Pete. The second is that this office is grossly overstaffed." She strode towards Joe's office.

"By fully fifty per cent. British management is rightly criticised for its excessive fat and featherbedding."

It was Joe's good fortune that he'd shut his office door, and that the wild rattle of the handle allowed him to replace the telephone in time, for Jane in fury was a sight for which nothing in his pleasant life had prepared him; but, in his last scrap of self-possession, he knew he should speak first, and said:

"I've been offered a partnership at Price Waterhouse, Jane. I meant to tell you, but you've been so busy."

"Will you reconsider?"

"It's a good opportunity for me, Jane."

"All right. You've done some good work here, notably over the refinancing of the demerger mortgages. I'll write to the senior partner of Price Waterhouse and say that. You can have a year's salary as a leaving bonus. Is that fair, Joe?"

"Very fair, Jane."

"You are free to go whenever it is convenient to you and Price Waterhouse."

In reality, of course, Jane needed a finance director no more than she needed a secretary. They were merely company. For Jane was lonely. She looked at her watch: six in the morning in California. Let him sleep an hour more.

Stephen saw that, although she was asleep among empty Coke cups and cold Chinese food, much of her was alert; and that, if he stood up and crossed the carpet under the fluorescent light and touched her electric hair, she'd blink and put her lovely long hands around his neck, or one on his neck and one on his belt; then stand and step out of her dress, as if born to it; as if she were a piece of darkness, reserved from the night he'd lost and holding all its sweetness and security and rest; and it's happened before, in the boardroom of Keeling Mann, happened all the time in fact and most often at this moment when the Pacific light comes rolling in though the blinds and you hear the Freeway roar; and she's thought about it, because she wants a man more than power or fame or money, some women are funny like that.

"Steve?"

"Donna?"

She raised her head from the table. "What's wrong with you British guys?"

Stephen brought his cup of whisky and his cigarette to the table. He said: "Donna, sometimes I can't stand straight when I'm around you."

"So do something about it."

"I have commitments, Donna."

"Sure do."

"Donna, you just can't get off one moving train and on to another going the other way."

She yawned. "Well, this train's going to be gone soon." Her sleepy eyes narrowed on his cigarette. "Hey, this is a no-smoking state. You want the gas-chamber, dumbo." And then, crinkling her nose: "Gimme. Now."

Stephen handed her the last of the joint. She said, through garlands of smoke: "Jane care for this guy? The guy we're picking up."

Stephen stretched.

"I asked a fucking question."

"I guess."

There, thought Stephen: that wasn't that hard, was it?

"And you care for Jane?"

"I redid §67c. It's fine now."

"You got a problem, boy."

"Shall we get back to work?"

She said: "I never was on a train, Steve."

"Donna! §67c!"

She banged her hand on the table. Her poise and wit fell off her. She looked hard-used, defeated. "I just want some fucking happiness in my life."

Stephen reached out to touch her hair, but she shook her head.

"OK. It's OK. I'm fine. Let's get on. What is this shit?"

And so on.

142

Jane, though distant from this room by an ocean and continent, existed in the same moment; and, as she stood by her window over Burlington Street, London, the moment pierced her. She felt herself to be falling through the cold air, not from her gravity, but from a loss of light, like a spark from an extinguished roman candle. She did not know what had been said, and could not have imagined it. She felt no pleasure at her friend's happiness. But she was flooded by relief that she was again, as in her earliest years, alone.

Jane left the Burlington Street office by the back door and was driven to South London in a Jaguar with dark windows, an unheard-of extravagance compounded in that she kept it idle in Streatham High Street while she conducted the following interview.

"You can't go in there. The General Secretary . . ."

Jane walked on past Sheila Wright; but as she put her hand to the door, it opened, and a small man was standing in it. He was of an ugliness that stopped Jane dead in her steps. He was perhaps five feet two inches, with a heavy bald head that slid without interruption of neck into a tedious shirt and suit, with small, intelligent eyes and a mouth that seemed to have curled under a permanent heat of contempt. The man was tight, balled-up, either with intellectual energy or violence, Jane couldn't tell. She felt ice in her blood. He stood back for her:

"Jane Bellarmine, I assume."

As she entered, Jane turned, to make some gesture of conciliation to the woman, and saw, in Sheila's whole person, the fear and resentment of a mistreated pet.

He moved across and sat down behind a clean desk. There was nothing on the walls and no furniture, but a set of kitchen chairs, one of which Jane took. As she sat down, he said: "I know the country about Wexley Park. Our College of Marxist Education is at . . ."

"I didn't come here to talk about country estates, Mr McVie. Also, I like to be known as Miss Haddon or Jane or any combination of the two."

McVie waved his hand: as if to say, You have good reason to be frightened of me, woman, but your aggression is puerile.

"I understand from *Workers Week*" – fear now made Jane ingratiating – "that a woman who says she is my half-sister is living at the house at Moresbydale. I would like to see this woman, either now or as soon as possible."

McVie took on what might have been intended as a smile. "For us, that is, for the Marxists, the working class is the privileged class because it feels on its back and hands and feet and in its belly the movements of history. The event interested us, not anecdotally, as it does the organs of bourgeois publicity, but because of its power to instruct. In a single family, and by family I include the squalid, degenerate and temporary associations typical of the lowest class of proletarians, there are two sisters: one accepts her potent inheritance, and attempts to master it through analysis and practice; the second flees in horror from its power and responsibility, to coquette with dukes on sunny terraces, consume fine wines, wear costly dresses; and when the manifest contradictions of such a fatuous existence become apparent even to her befuddled brain, she assumes the mask of the oppressors, uses the only valuable knowledge she has – her class consciousness – to wound and smear the class embodied by her sister. For us, Jane, there is no morality except class morality as reflected . . ."

Jane interrupted him. McVie had not been interrupted, except by the thugs of the orthodox Communist Party and the other Trotskyite sects, for thirty-one years: since, to be precise, Khrushchev's secret speech to the XXth Congress of the Communist Party of the Soviet Union, when tormented and homeless comrades streamed in their dozens, even scores, to the party of the working class, where they immediately were obliged to submit to the most rigid democratic centralism or rather the will of Sean McVie at any historical conjuncture. McVie, who did not at first understand what was happening, heard Jane speaking, very angrily, and was suddenly satisfied with himself, at his own tolerance within the framework of a scrupulously analysed and vigilantly defended ideology. He recognised that he could be impatient with the views of women, and that this must be mastered through a disciplined sympathy. Perhaps, he thought, this child, with her high and misapplied intelligence, by means of a thorough and comradely indoctrination in the correct analysis of her bourgeois existence, might yet be captured for the class struggle!

This is what Jane said: "It is precisely because I come from the working class, or rather that debased component of it that does not even merit the name of working class, that QE Works is fortunate to be my responsibility. You have made a profound error, Mr McVie, both of common sense and, in as much as I understand these things, historical materialist theory. Having fomented a strike at Motherwell, you must now take its consequences, which are these: I shall be relieved of my job, the new automated line will not be built but rather the workforce will be dismissed with one month's pay for each year of seniority, and the process plant dismantled and shipped abroad, probably to Bangalore in Southern India. At some stage, though not in this business cycle, the building will be knocked down and the site redeveloped, possibly for an industrial purpose but not employing those women, who will never work for wages again except, conceivably, as domestic servants. That is substantially all your doing, Mr McVie."

McVie was silent, as if to reveal to her the error of interruption: as if to say, I wish to ensure you have no more to say, before I rebut your analysis.

He said at last: "The fate of a single industrial object is of importance in so far, not as it provides profits for the owners of its productive capital or a miserable existence to its wage-dependants, but as it reveals to the working class and its allies the actual relations of production. Class struggle is a process of education. I would have thought, Jane, that the working class of England and Scotland will draw some conclusions from the frivolous destruction of this factory; and, turning to your case, from the extreme unwisdom of class disaffiliation. Now, you spoke about this woman, whose name I believe is Cathy McKay. I am prepared to accompany you to the college, to permit you to meet this woman in private, and also to leave you together, if that is your wish and her wish. I must merely ask you to drive, since I do not."

He stood up. He seemed to have grown in bulk and assumed a terrifying authority. Jane began to tremble uncontrollably. She said: "I will not permit you to injure me."

She saw, in a flash, that this had happened before, happened all the time, all those girls in charity-shop jackets, those extras from the Gaiety swept up by the Equity group, those orphans from Sidon and Beit Jennine; so many girls, so many girls; brought round by Sheila in tightly buttoned rage and up the stairs, and to the sofa and a mug of tea; and as they understand, really understand, for the first time, that first paragraph of the *Eighteenth Brumaire*, its great phrases throbbing with a new vision of human affairs, they look at you with eyes glistening like November streets; and, at that moment, you know in the depths of your being that these girls, these bonny girls, are more veritable than the great tides of history, more *dialectical* than the Transitional Programme; and you explode in rage and shame, and the shock stays in their eyes for the rest of their lives.

McVie was coming round the desk, carrying a briefcase. Jane saw that she was standing behind her chair. She said: "Don't come nearer, or I'll destroy you, McVie. I'll reveal to the bourgeois press that you have had sexual relations with young female party comrades, and comrades from foreign sections of the Fourth International, over more than thirty years, and numbering several hundreds; several hundred lives blighted beyond repair; and that the Central Committee of the Workers Party both knew about and connived at this abuse of your patriarchal power. If you let me go now, alone, to my sister, and desist from these abuses, I shall keep this secret. I give you my word and I have never broken it."

McVie was halted. For the first time since his earliest youth in Kirkcaldy and on the Clyde, he was speechless. He looked to Jane old now, ready to die soon. He said:

"An antique smear of the Security Service, of no consequence to . . ."

"Well, no doubt, Mrs Rimington will also have fabricated sufficient evidence. I imagine it will take me half a morning to assemble it."

McVie let out his breath. "She has left the college, against my wishes. I believe she is now under the control of one of the bourgeois newspapers. My assistant knows the name of it."

"There's so much hatred in you, Sean McVie. What happened to you? What did they do to you, Sean McVie, over all those years? And it's nearly over, and where is your revolution: just fifteen hundred members, six hundred of them in arrears, some odd jobs for the Iraqis and an old man and a terrorised woman in a dingy office off Streatham High Street."

McVie looked away. He said: "Revolution occurs in objective historical circumstances, that appear not to have coincided with my lifetime. That is not my doing, but the operation of history. Leon Davidovich said to me, in Mexico just before he was murdered by the State Fascists: 'The career of the revolutionary requires a superhuman sacrifice, McVie. Merely committed people will fail.' I have discovered I am merely human, and now also mortal. The struggle continues. It would help you if you understood that, Jane."

Jane left the room and descended to the street, where her carriage was waiting.

11

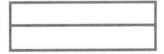

They walked back together across the garden, the elk-hound making wide circles around them, always in sight, as if on some tether of familiarity; but anger seemed to exhaust Elizabeth Bellarmine, made her breathless and heavy in her movement. The big house grew bigger to Jane with the pettifogging slowness of a nightmare. She tried one more time.

"Excuse me . . ."

"I wish you would stop saying excuse me, Jane. We are not on a bus."

Jane didn't have another shot.

"And do stop calling me Lady Bellarmine, if you possibly can."

How the Countess wanted Jane to address her is quite unclear to me, for it surely wasn't as Elizabeth. There was, I suppose, another possible address and this fell on Jane with such weight it was as if the house and park and trees had been dropped on her; but Lady Bellarmine was away on the wings of her frustration.

She said: "If I don't know who you are, dear Jane, how can I love you?" She looked on Jane with a rhetorical smile, that had disabled hundreds in its time, men and women; and that, I regret to say, Jane remembered and stocked in her expanding armoury.

In her distress, Jane could still see there was something wrong with the question, and had this thought: Your son doesn't try to know. But she dared not say such a thing, as if she feared it went to the heart of the business and the whole place – house, garden, dog, park, woods – would explode; and anyway the thought had at last occurred to Elizabeth Bellarmine or rather had been there all the time but had been ignored, like a well-informed wine-waiter or a guest expert in pictures, until it had become so insistent that something had to be done.

Lady Bellarmine pulled herself together, a procedure which had its physical aspect. She put her stick in front her, leaned on it and tested, then defeated, the pain in her back. She said: "Kiss me, Jane." Which Jane did, quickly and without tears, for she did not want to strain the Countess's resolution.

"There was a lady there . . ."

"It doesn't matter."

"She . . . she . . ."

"Sshh."

They continued towards the mountainous house. Lady Bellarmine said: "I would like to adopt you, Jane, if you will allow me and regardless of what you and Johnny . . ."

"Oh, why?"

"Why?" The Countess felt her exasperation rise again. She stopped walking. "I rather thought it would help you to have some property as well as your education. The world can be a . . ."

"Please don't. There'll be nothing left of me." She stared round wildly, scattering tears. Windows. Fountain. Obelisk. Sea. The Countess of Bellarmine. The prancing dog.

At that moment, Lady Bellarmine thought: I am too old to go to school at the hands of this girl. She should have said, I'm so sorry, Jane; she came to it; but she was a stiff-necked woman; it was her fault and she knew it. And in the hall, where they took off their boots and dried the unexhausted dog, and she thought: She'll go off to her room to sulk or read, what a bore, and I must lie down where all the ladders start, she did nothing to hold Jane but strode to her sitting room and wrote eight business letters till Johnny came in with the glass of whisky she had at a quarter-past-seven every evening and had had since the evening of Omaha Beach.

"I hope," she said, without looking up, "that you intend to treat that girl fairly."

Johnny, who knew his mother, ignored the question and looked instead for the distress in her that it represented. He said: "Mum, you could have been a scholar at Oxford, if you'd wanted to."

Lady Bellarmine was mollified to the extent of taking her glass. She said, mostly to herself: "I worry about not what she's gained there, but what she lost."

Johnny had never heard his mother use the words I worry. "Have you guys had a row?"

Lady Bellarmine did not have rows. She said: "I wonder why young people don't get on with it. You've known each other long enough."

Long enough was three weeks and if, as Johnny thought, his mother knew he'd proposed marriage to Jane twenty-five minutes after he'd met her, then she'd stop tormenting him! In this, he was wholly mistaken: for Elizabeth Knollys had slept with her husband-to-be at their first meeting, and in a Free French Daimler outside the Chatham Dockyard and before any proposal or acceptance. I repeat this scandal, simply to record the truth that no generation has a monopoly of sex, else we'd long ago have vanished from the earth; and if you think ill of the Countess for her hypocrisy in matters of sex, you should know she justified it to herself, rather unsatisfactorily, as that being what you did in wartime, when each evening might be his last or yours; and though she knew, from common sense rather than Kant, that all right actions should be transmutable into objective moral laws, she also sensed it was right to treat each moment as your last, and this was also religious; for which you will no doubt think her a very muddled person.

"Mum."

They knew each other, loved each other, and had manoeuvred themselves, by long tactical experience, to a place where they could not fight: where the ground was impassable to wheeled traffic or the lines were separated by thick woodland.

"Well, you must do what you like, my darling."

This sentence, with its barbaric mixture of the imperative and the voluntary, was often a signal for truce between them. But Elizabeth Bellarmine, rising to join her son on the sofa, felt something in her that was not to be budged: something more than anger, or envy of Jane or jealousy of her or love for her; something that would accompany her the rest of her life; something cold.

She got up from the sofa. "I suppose I'd better go and make sure she's all right."

Johnny felt his universe shiver. He thought he'd built his world on his mother's rigidity, but in his heart he must have feared she was brittle, and that's why he'd always given in to her; and now the brittleness was revealed in this apology to him, the best she'd ever manage, in regret and love and fear of death.

"Oh for God's sake, Mum."

Elizabeth Bellarmine turned at the door, smiling. "She is, after all, our guest." The bell for dinner rang.

Johnny said: "Do we have a Shakespeare?"

"We have a folio, darling. Dad bought it from Mr Morgan in New York. Do you need it?"

"If you could tell me where it is . . ."

"Certainly not. I'll get it down for you."

Johnny found Jane lying on her bed, barefoot and dressed, and reading. When he came in, she rose like a charmed snake, dropping the book and the envelope she used to separate the lines of type, and looked at him with cautious eyes. He thought: Don't drop anything for me, it's not wise or safe; but he kissed her all the same.

"Johnny! It's dinner!"

"This won't take a moment."

"I'm starving!"

"I just need you to lie down. You may feel some minor discomfort in the . . ."

And so on.

And then she wouldn't let him go. She said into his shirt: "Eating. Reading. Fucking. I can't tell the difference any more. My appetites are all muddled up."

Johnny stood up and found her tights and shoes.

"Is that what people mean, Johnny? When they talk about happiness?"

"I think we should go down."

At the top of the stairs, he said: "Do you want to get married?"

"Yes, please."

"I mean now."

"Yes."

Johnny sighed. He said: "We'll tell Mum after dinner. She's very fond of you, Jane. You should realise that."

But there was no dinner at Wexley Park that night.

Jane was left alone in a house ticking with clocks. She read in the library and went to the Countess's sitting room each morning at ten, though sometimes she glanced at the square chairs side by side at the desk, but they were empty, and she looked back down at Graham & Dodds' *Principles of Balance-Sheet Analysis*. In the dining room, she tried to talk about her reading and the weather while Johnny and his sisters, who had come up from Sheffield and London respectively, stared smiling at infinity.

Meanwhile, Elizabeth Bellarmine slipped out of consciousness.

Half-way through the next week, Jane managed to catch him at the head of the stairs. He listened with intense interest. After a while, he said:

"But where would you go?"

"I can have my room at college. I telephoned, if you don't mind."

Johnny straightened. He said: "I wonder, Jane, if you could bear to stay here a little longer."

The next morning, Jane sensed the shadow of a conspiracy. The sisters, who up to then had treated her courteously, made absent gestures of consideration, rising to get the Burgundy from the sideboard to fill her empty glass while Johnny was staring, or crossing the Slings to join her as she walked the Countess's demoralised dog to the obelisk. Scraps of conversation stuck to her. "So why on earth can't Jane be there," she heard Meg say, exasperated.

At breakfast, while she was helping herself to more black pudding behind a screen, Johnny said: "It's none of her business, can't you see?" and it pierced her, so her knees buckled by the hot plate.

At four the next morning, light came through the doorway of her bedroom, then vanished. Jane sat up. He was sitting at the end of the bed.

"How are you, Jane?"

How are *you*?

"Where are you, Jane?"

Here.

He didn't touch her.

Jane began to tremble. "I can't. I can't. Please don't make me go in there! Johnny, please don't make me!"

He held her against his shirt-front. "Don't worry. Don't worry about anything."

She stood up, quaking. She groped for her dressing-gown. "It's just . . . It's just . . ."

"I know, Jane. You're very brave. My mum was so proud of you." He turned his head away. "She's gone now. She sent her love."

Jane fell through his hands to the floor.

"The door," she screamed. "*Die Tür . . . Sie hat versucht, die Tür . . .*"

She began to crawl towards the corner of the room.

"Stop it, Jane! Enough!"

She was balled into the corner, ghostly in her night-gown.

"*Eigentlich hat sie versucht, . . . die Tür . . . Sie . . .*"

"*Ruhe, Ruhe, du Arme.*"

Jane cannot remember the first occasion she had heroin; only the sensation, which seemed to her like happiness. She was stoned at their wedding that November (Marylebone Registry Office, Stephen and Vijay only).

So. 1980. Somewhere in England. Whizzing between mown fields. Etcetera.

Johnny Bellarmine craned over at the speedometer and saw it read 110 miles per hour. He said: "Jane, there might be other people or animals on the road. You should slow down."

Jane, who did not always ignore the clearly expressed will of her husband, put her foot on the brake. The wheels of the Bentley, not surprisingly, locked and the car swerved off the road and bounced along with two wheels in the ditch. Jane thought: Beside any smooth progress is this bumping, which will be mine for the rest of my life: bump, bump, bump and then smash. Johnny thought: I need to get the speed down.

The car hit a little bridge over the ditch, reared up, and then came on to the road again. The wheels, unlocked, began to gather speed again in the direction of a big oak on the far side of the road. Johnny pulled on the handbrake and the car spun once, then twice, then a third time. Jane thought: Whee, like dancing. Johnny thought: We're down to sixty, we're in at the weights. Let's hit, why not, with the boot, nothing in there but wine and fags. He leaned over and put one hand on Jane's face and the other against her neck.

The car hit at the front passenger door which threw him on to her. This, I believe, prevented her neck being broken, though at the cost to Johnny of an extreme pain in the ankle he left behind. The windows starred and then fell outwards, letting in a blast of twilight. The engine stayed where it belonged. Things ground and creaked and complained.

"Out, Jane. Now. Try and stand up."

He pushed her through the window and followed himself, trailing his new foot. She looked in misery at the ruined car. She wasn't cut. He tested his foot on the gravel surface. Well, he didn't faint, so he must have been all right.

"Oh, Johnny, I'm so sorry. I'll replace it, I promise."

"Sshh," he said, putting his arm round her. "It's only a car. You should lie down and keep warm."

He led her into the back seat. The doors had conveniently sprung. Through the peaked boot, he found, by eleven intact bottles of Château Beychevelle 1959, a tartan rug which he spread over her.

"On your front, Jane."

She lay with her face to the back of the seat.

"Does anything hurt, Jane?"

"No. Must be the gear."

"You are very fortunate you were stoned, because otherwise you would be dead."

"But what about *you*, Johnny?"

"I'm fine." He lay down against her back and said this: "I'm afraid, Jane, that you need help. More than I can give you. You will kill yourself or me, and either would be a crime. Do you understand?"

From the depths of the seat leather and her shivering junkie misery, Jane nodded.

"We might not get another chance."

"It's that you don't love me!"

"I do. It's simply that . . ." He took a breath. "I was upset when my mother died. I didn't realise how much she protected me." He smiled at her back. "Also, my darling, you ought to know that injecting heroin is not a particularly winning habit in a young woman."

"I only do it because you won't fuck me!"

"Well, I will now. Do stop fussing, Jane."

"Help!"

He lifted her ballgown to her hips. Jane's heart sang. She tore at the front of her dress to bare her breast. It had annoying little hooks and eyes and she decided, given the relative rewards on offer, to rip them. As he came into her, she felt more complete than after the best of bestest hits. She thought: I'll get clean in New York, in a new place. She began to feel intolerably tight and fragile. Her body raced away from her, leaving just a residue of unbearable regret.

"Thanks," he said.

"You won't move, will you."

"I won't move."

"Tell me about Meg and Johnny. You promised you would one day."

"Well, she was milking with the other girls in the cow-shed . . ."

"As it is now?"

"Pretty much, except there were girls instead of the machine. And he came in . . ."

"Johnny! Please, don't. Please."

Johnny stopped whatever he was doing.

"Alone?"

"Doesn't say. My father never had time for things like this but my mother went around after the War, asking all the old people like Mary Edgcombe's mum, you know, the people who couldn't read and so still thought in the old way. It may not be what happened, but it's how the people remembered it, which means it had a meaning for them. It's a story. Do you understand the difference?"

"Suck eggs, Johnny."

"In the circumstances . . ."

"Sshh! Go on."

"He asked her to draw him some milk."

"What does that mean?"

"Oh come on, Jane!"

"What does it mean?"

"What we've just done."

"I see. And was it a usual thing to say? Or an interesting thing to say? What does the story think of it?"

Johnny thought for a moment. "Not normal, for a Christian house in Northern England. The story's saying Johnny was very wrong. Unless of course . . ."

"Unless what?"

"She was already ruined."

"What does that mean?"

"That she was going promiscuously with men."

"Was she?"

"No. But she seems to have been heading that way."

"What stopped her?"

"The events of the story. Which also stopped Johnny from going to the bad."

"How did she answer him?"

"She said: 'Draw it yourself, sir.'"

"What does that mean?"

"Jane, are you being deliberately obtuse?"

"No. I need to hear it from you."

"Well, if you don't know, I'm not telling you."

"All right, I can guess. Why's that in the story?"

"I suppose to show she was lippy. Sixteen-year-old cowgirls didn't talk like that to lords in the eighteenth-century."

"Does the story think she was right to say that?"

"No. I think very, very wrong. That she was almost a bad hat. But sure of herself, sure of something. Her face, I suppose."

"She might have been very bright."

"We can't know because she died. But she couldn't read when they married. Johnny's mother had to teach her. And the spelling in her letters, even by eighteenth-century standards . . ."

"That doesn't mean anything."

The questions, the shock of the smash, and the intense intimacy between them, exhausted Johnny. He said: "Maybe you're right. Maybe she'd felt him looking at her in the shed or rick-yard, felt his love on her, felt her love for him. We can't know."

"What happened next?"

"Johnny went away and came back in his uniform . . ."

"Immediately?"

"Doesn't say. Maybe it was over days. She'd always be there for the afternoon milking."

"His Navy lieutenant's uniform?"

"No. Another. In those days, at some houses, there was a coat that all the men wore, a sort of house uniform."

"What colour was yours?"

"Ours? Indigo blue. Johnny bought the indigo in Savannah."

"Where's that?"

"Georgia, in the US."

"And why did he put it on?"

"It was the proposal."

"I see."

"So he stood by her stall, looking down the back end of an eighteenth-century cow, and offered her his arm."

"Indigo blue arm?"

"Yes."

"And what did Meg do?"

"She said she had to finish her milking."

"Why does the story have her do that?"

"Many reasons. First, because the cow needed to be milked, and it would make work for one of the other girls if she left off. Second, because the cow was her job, her only job. Third, probably, to make the other girls laugh. They were her friends, and they weren't going to get another chance to make fun of their lord. And also for a better reason, which makes me think you're right and she was clever: to show him that even she, an illiterate milkmaid, was giving something up for him."

"And then what?"

"He stood, among the cows and laughing girls. And I doubt it was shy giggles. Country girls didn't giggle in the eighteenth-century. And then Meg told him to go and wait in the rick-yard."

"As it is now?"

"Pretty much; but I should think much, much dirtier. Rob Cato is a pretty good cowman . . ."

"Why?"

"Why does the story have her tell him to?"

"Yes."

"Perhaps to test whether he really could take an order from her. She may not have been that sure of herself. And, I think, to protect him. It can't have been easy for him, standing there by a cow's arse end, with all those dirty jokes and innuendoes flying over the steaming backs at him. Maybe a jet of milk hit his coat. Though he was only twenty-one, he'd already fought three pitched battles. He'd been under the cliffs at Quebec, taking in the landing party, which must have been quite something. He'd spent two days and a night under Princess Pacioli's bed in Genoa, living on *amaretti* kicked by housemaids under the valance, while her husband turned the city upside down, impounded the ship, hanged the purser. I think it was hard for him, perilous, like throwing away his weapon or trying to surrender."

"And why did he go and wait in the rick-yard?"

"What do you mean? Because he loved her."

"That's not the reason for the story. What does this part mean? Why do they remember it this way, and not another?"

"Oh, right. I think to show that he was ready to make a sacrifice for her. Literally, to take shit. Otherwise, the marriage couldn't have worked."

"It didn't."

"Impossible as you may find this to imagine, you're wrong, Jane. And the family memory, and the memory in the district, is that this was something very special, not an ordinary marriage."

"Why would he have to take shit for her? Because she was a cow maid?"

"No. For another reason."

"That she was actually or potentially a bad hat?"

"Yes, Jane."

"So what happened next?"

"Meg picked up her stool and went out alone into the rick-yard."

"Please, Johnny, one thing at a time."

"I imagine the stool was her only piece of property, except her dress and apron and cap and underlinen. So she would take it with her to her husband."

"Oh dear, Johnny."

"Don't blame me."

She wriggled away from him, and turned round. "You didn't keep it! You keep every damn thing of Johnny's down to his fucking stores books. Yet you won't keep Meg's only property! Just because she's a woman."

"Do shut up, Jane, and come back here. You are an opinionated and sentimental toad. My mother kept it in her sitting room. With the indigo cushion with the coronet."

Jane said nothing. He took her back, and turned her onto her front again.

"Please go on."

"She went out of the shed, to show she had stopped working

160

for wages. And into the rick-yard alone, because that accepted his proposal."

"Alone?"

"Out of kindness, because her friends weren't going to be ladies, and also because it was now none of their business."

"And did they go straight to church?"

"Doesn't say. I very much doubt it. I think they went into the hay-loft and did what we've just done, while the girls peered through the knot-holes at the blood on her thighs, till Johnny stood up and scared them, cackling, away. They might as well have had some fun. There wasn't much fun to be had in the eighteenth-century, even for lords and ladies. Anyway, there was nothing wrong, the marriage was signed and sealed before numerous witnesses."

"I don't understand."

"I now see that's the point of the story: it's a contract of marriage, in more or less legal form, probably already fixed in the form that my mum heard, but not in written form, since nobody knew how to write. It guarantees Meg's rights in the marriage, not before a court of law, but before the district, which in those days may have been more important."

"Was that usual?"

"I should think unique."

"So why was the story made and remembered?"

"Because of some special quality . . ."

"In Johnny?"

"No. I think in Meg."

"Say it, Johnny."

"Meg had no surname. My mother said that's not at all uncommon for Northumberland at that period."

"Please say what you have to say."

Johnny sighed. "She must have been somehow under the protection of the dale, inasmuch as that was a social entity at that time."

"Why? What was wrong with her family?"

"Jane, she can't have had any kin. Otherwise, it doesn't make sense."

Jane said nothing.

"The story is a contract between the district and my family that she not be mistreated."

"Was your family unpopular then?"

"Jane, the question makes no sense. My family owned the county. The relations of power were all in our favour."

Jane said nothing.

"The marriage made my family popular. That's why we've prospered here for two hundred and twenty years."

She reached round with her arm and pulled him towards her.

Johnny said: "Did you know the answers?"

"Only if you did."

"It's nice, the story, isn't it? Sexy."

"Not as sexy as you in my tum. Please finish the story for me."

"It's finished."

"But as you'd tell it."

"Well, it got cold, though she had the indigo coat over her. So she put on her dress and he carried her over the rick-yard and to the house. And the housekeeper shrieked in her night-cap, and the footmen slunk away, and they strode, arm in arm, down the passage to the drawing-room. And Mrs Moran . . ."

"She can't have been called Mrs Moran . . ."

" . . .well Mrs Somebody ran up with a sponge for her face, and the housemaids tried to slip on shoes and a bonnet and a ribbon for her waist, but she kicked the shoes off, and Johnny knocked the bonnet flying and the girl with the ribbon just stood, in the candlelight, marvelling. The double doors flew open and behind the column . . ."

"As it is now . . ."

"Just as it is now . . ."

"She took his hand behind the column, then let go and they walked into the room."

"What was his mother doing?"

"Viscountess Bellarmine was at that little desk by the fire going over the mine accounts with the Supervisor and the Manager. Her maid was plaiting her hair. The Secretary was reading to her from Adam Smith's *Theory of Moral Sentiments*, which had arrived that evening by the post, a present from Hume. She looked up, in her cap and pince-nez. She signalled quickly to the men, who bowed to her, to her son and to the girl in dirty clothes. Grizel Bellarmine tried to get up, but her stick had slipped from her chair. Johnny said:

"'Madame, may I present my Meg?'

Meg bobbed a curtsey.

Lady Bellarmine tried again to get up, and this time was helped by her maid.

"'Do you like my son, Meg?'

"'Yes, m'lady.' Bob.

"'How old are you, Meg?'

"'I don't know, m'lady.' Bob.

"'Can you read, Meg?'

"'No, m'lady.' Bob.

"'You will come to me tomorrow at ten o'clock to learn reading. Mrs Moran!'"

"'Johnny, she can't have been called Mrs Moran!'"

"Mrs Whatever! 'You will prepare Miss Meg a bed in my dressing-room and show her every consideration.'

"'Yes, m'lady.' Bob.

"'Please kiss your mother, Miss Meg.'"

"Did she?"

"She did, so tight you'd think nothing could separate them. And as Meg left with Mrs Whatnot, she gave Johnny a look of utter despair."

"Because she wasn't much interested in marriage. Only in fucking."

"As it were, Jane."

"And what did the maid do?"

"She whispered something in her mistress's ear."

"But the old lady told her to shut up?"

"I'm afraid Lady Bellarmine slapped her maid."

"And what about Johnny?"

"It was the only occasion where he wanted to strangle his beloved mother."

"So what did he do?"

"Well, he talked to the head gardener about planting a creeper he had brought back from Charleston outside his mother's window."

"What did the gardener make of it?"

"Well, I think the whole district felt for their plight."

"Why didn't that work?"

"Because the ladder broke, and dislocated Johnny's arm. That's why he's a bit lop-sided in the Batoni portrait."

"And what did Meg do?"

"She did English, French, Spanish, sewing, dancing, singing and double-entry book-keeping. All day, every day except Sunday."

"So they met on Sunday?"

"At church."

"What happened there?"

"As they came down from their pews, they passed twists of paper into each other's hands."

"What did they say?"

"His, scrawled, said: I am dying for my Meg. Hers, in laborious clerk's script said: My lord, Onored as Ey Am by Your Regard, and That of Your Laidy Mother, Ey Would Be Relived Before God, If the Day of Our Blessed Yunion were To-day or To-morry and Atendant on Our Love Not on My Speling yr affect. servant Margaret Bellarmine."

"Poor Meg!"

"Poor Johnny!"

"So what happened?"

"Conflans broke out of Brest."

"Who? What?"

"French admiral. Forty-three sail. Johnny was gazetted Post-Captain and called to the *Fléchette*, fifty-four guns, at The Nore."

"What about Meg? What did Meg do?"

"Meg took action."

"She said she was pregnant!"

Johnny said: "No, Jane."

"What did Meg do?"

"They were going over the overseas accounts. She said:

"'May I speak, m'lady.' Bob.

"'Speak, my darling.'

"'May we be wed to-day, m'lady.' Bob.

"Grizel Bellarmine smiled and said: 'It will be all the sweeter for you, my sugar, once you understand the administration of the Barbadoes farms. Your fellow's no business-man.'

"'May I speak, m'lady.' Bob.

"'Speak, my duck.'

"'He will be drownded in the waves!'

"Johnny's mother said nothing.

"'May I speak, m'lady?'

"'You may not.'

"'I feel a piece of coldness on me . . .'"

"Johnny don't!"

"'. . . and I do not know how long I can serve My Lord and Thee, my Mother.'

"'Mrs Moran! Where is that ignorant woman! Mrs Moran! These children will be married! At three to-day! For it is God's will!' And, Jane, can't you hear the farmers scrambling down the fell, and the neighbours pounding the bad roads on their second-best horses, and the womenfolk grumbling, stuck in carts in the mud in their bonnets, and the bells ringing out hour after hour."

"And was it fun, the wedding, Johnny? Was it fun?"

"Not at first. Because Meg and Johnny went straight from Wexley Church to the bedroom, the one that's now called Huahine, that Omsai slept in after the Fourth Voyage, you know, and she bounced on the bed so her wedding-dress flew up with her hair. And they stayed there three hours, fighting and weeping and making love, while the farmers ate and ate and drank and drank and the neighbours computed the income of the estate to the last guinea; till finally, at nine, they came down the stairs, she so sad she could scarcely walk, and smiled, and went down the line, and tenants thought: Bonny lass, and neighbours thought: *Charmante*! And they went into the ballroom and danced, whee! all night and most of morning."

"I'll always love you, Johnny."

"Sshh."

There is, in addition, a piece of evidence from Clutterbuck's *Diaries*, though these were suppressed by Elizabeth Bellarmine, and neither Johnny nor Jane was aware of this citation. It is in an entry for 11 June, 1782:

> Also present were some Gentlemen in uniform, including Lord B–, a Captain in the Royal Navy and a very pretty young man. The family had been long established at Wexley Hall, in the County of Northumberland, where a number of Coal-mines were worked on the Estate; and needing to transport this mineral to markets in the Low Countries and at London, My Lord's family became Engaged in Ship-Building and Commerce at Newcastle, where they displayed a Sagacity in Business not generally found among our Landed-Men. The young man, known to the district as Young Johnny to distinguish him from his father, the Great Navigator, with whom he sailed at age six as what they call a Servant, is rich even by the measure of these Northern Magnates. His fortune, and his pretty face, made him the object of lively interest to certain Ladies. But discovering that the Captain's interest lay in sea-fights, and freights and demurrage and Arctic whalefishes, the Fair ones withdrew and sought more Fashionable Diversion. It is said that his posthumous mother, who was prettily painted by Rosalba in the character of a Milk-maid, was indeed such a servant and that her mother followed a yet more Antient Profession. But I cannot credit these stories, even for the Northern part of our Kingdom.

Also this, from Li Po, which Johnny did know and repeated to himself:

Fortunate is the man who contemplates his ancestors, for he shall become wise.

She turned round at him. "Johnny, I want us to divorce."

"There's no such thing as divorce. You haven't been listening, have you?"

"Do as I ask, please."

"Why?"

"So I can hurt you. So everybody will know what sort of man you are, that you aren't a man at all, because you can't love anybody. And as we go through life, everything I do will wound you. Every time you enter a room, conversation will fall away. There'll be trickles of laughter. As I grow, so you will diminish. I'll be well-known and powerful and happy, and you will be ridiculous, and every time you hear of me, it will be like a stab in your heart. And . . ."

She sat up, tugged at her hair. The Bellarmine tiara lay where it had fallen in drifts of sweet-papers and shivered glass. She tore at Meg's earrings. Johnny reached out and held her wrist.

"Stop that."

Jane stopped.

"I'm so sorry, Jane."

"It's not your fault, it's . . ." She started in fear.

"I meant about your mum."

"Shut up. Leave me alone, damn you."

She tried to scramble up the back seat.

"Some time, you'll have to go back."

She went for his eyes, but he got his hand up, and her nails scratched across the back of his hand.

He held her arms. She tried to get her knee up between his legs, but he kneeled on her, till she was still. The pain in his broken foot made him want to strangle her.

She said: "The girls used to say it at school. I wasn't popular."

Johnny let her go, experimentally. He sat up, against the back seat.

"I won't." She began to tremble again.

"You will, because I will make you. Not now. Not this year. Not next year. But you have to go, or you will never be happy or make anybody happy; and if you have a child, you will transfer your misery to that child." Johnny had no idea what he was saying until he said it. He felt he was groping down a street with only the faint and intermittent light of her intelligence, and his own, like cracked street-lamps. "Go to New York. Make yourself famous or whatever, and then come back. I'll still be here."

Johnny stopped, because Jane wasn't listening. Part of her, he thought, was already in America, detoxified, anonymous, free. Part of her was on its slow journey north. Time to leave, softy! The dawn light hurt his eyes. He stood up.

"Jane, I'm going now to that village to call. Try and sleep. There's some more of that wine in the boot. You've got fags."

Jane was dreaming. She turned on him a look of heart-stopping tenderness. She said: "It'll just be a while, Johnny, you understand. Not for ever."

"I know."

But Johnny, who walked eight miles on his broken foot to the little town of Ashbourne in Derbyshire, did not believe it would be just for a while. For all the faith he'd taken from his mother at the price of those acres and millions, he did not believe he would ever again hold Jane in his arms in this world, or in the next; and that her sufferings in childhood, and in their short association, were too much for any person to bear even under a benign Providence. He did not know if she could save her life. He despaired of his own.

Jane was dreaming. Ships and water. A late November afternoon. Wind rising. A fast stern chase to leeward. An unsailed shore. How could she find an anchorage before the storm? The enemy would show her! And what would she do when she found that anchorage? Battle!

As the English line strung out in the roaring twilight, Hawke signalled from the flagship: "In the press and confusion of engagement, it shall not be possible to issue officers' instructions. Gentlemen in doubt shall know that none can do wrong that places his command alongside the enemy."

Fléchette, 54, newly careened at Chatham, came first into the bay. In the confined water, the French fleet could not deploy in line of battle, and she broke through the guard-ships and crossed under the stern of *Bellapais*, 74, the Marquis de la Levaille commanding. *Fléchette* took the French broadside in her rigging, lost her mizzen, and the mainmast topgallant, her boat and tiller and seventy sailors. In the speed of the chase, Johnny had brought up no ballast to barricade the quarter-deck. The second lieutenant took a ball in the throat, the mate lost his head to a round shot and Johnny was hit in the calf, jaw and back by ball and his left leg was broken by a falling top-sail spar. *Fléchette* fired on the down-roll and again on the up-roll. Johnny, who could not speak, signalled a halt to permit La Levaille to strike; but in the heavy sea, *Bellapais* listed and rolled into the gash in her gun-deck, came down on her beam ends, and sank in three-quarters of a minute, her colours draped over her taffrail.

That action, in view of both fleets, decided the outcome of the battle, spared England the inconvenience of French invasion, and made Jane a countess. But as she tossed in her bed of diamonds and glass, she thought to hear, from the floor of Quiberon Bay, the murmurs of five hundred and eighty boys and children; the clamour of uncounted cattle and sheep and chickens; the shrieks of seventeen contraband women; the agony of La Levaille; and she woke.

12

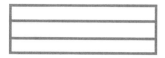

Jane stepped through the gates of the QE Works as if she were walking through cluster mines. The day-shift was coming out. The women streamed each side of her, looking away. Then somebody stopped and said:

"Will you lock us out, Jane?"

Jane looked up from the carpark tarmac. The women stopped and formed a mass about her. When she spoke, it was quietly, so they repeated it over their shoulders, rank by rank, till everybody had heard.

"I want you to know that if you vote for a strike, you will no longer deal with me. New management may be better for you, but it will be different. I want you to understand that."

"The strike vote was unanimous, Jane." An older woman, no doubt a machine foreman, said this.

Jane looked down again. "So that's that."

Somebody shouted: "You should work on that line, Jane. Then you'd know."

Jane said to her shoes: "I'd do the Basket without pay till I die, just to end this dispute."

"Cathy's a bad one, Jane. Don't believe a word she says." This was the older woman.

"She is also my sister, so you should take care what you say."

"Suit yourself."

"I need to go up the shops."

"What's he going to eat?"

"Who's going to get the kids from school?"

Jane raised her hand a little, as if in goodbye. Then the crowd opened, and she walked towards Jim Wallace's office.

Cathy McKay was sitting at a small round table of dented brass, with her knees together. She was smoking. It was eleven o'clock, and the sunny pub was all but empty. As Jane walked towards her, she threw her moussed hair out of her eyes. She looked round, suddenly, into the columns of glimmering dust, as if for a protector. Jane saw in Cathy's face her own face, but indistinctly – as if after many divergences out across the accidents of years, as railway lines, viewed from an InterCity window, split and race off and combine again in the course of a long journey. Her heart turned over.

"Hello, Cathy. I'm Jane."

"I'm not sorry about anything."

"You don't have to be sorry about anything." Jane reached out her hand and then lost her nerve and fiddled in her bag for her own cigarettes. "I'm so happy we've met at last. Can I sit down?"

Cathy McKay stared round, and then shifted a little on her sofa. She said: "You have to go to the world. The world don't come to you."

"Whatever it is, Cathy, it doesn't matter. How old are you?"

At that moment, a woman appeared at the table, in a city suit, replacing a phone card in her purse, smiling at Jane. She seemed to stand in some relation to the sisters, but of what sort Jane didn't know: only that she wasn't the bar-keep. "Are you Jane? Hi, I'm Madonna Consett, of *The Sun*. I'm working with Cathy on the story."

"What story?" Jane felt herself stiffen again, and made an effort to relax.

"You and Cathy, your mum, the mill, and all that. It's a great, great story, Jane! If we could maybe get you both outside, maybe at the main gate . . ."

"I wonder if you'd mind leaving us . . ."

"No," said Cathy.

"Cathy, I thought perhaps you could come down and stay with me in London for a few days, if you've got time. We could . . ."

"Is it true you're a junkie, Jane? You can tell me."

"Was. Not now. What about it, Cathy?"

"And you were sexually abused by your mother's clients?"

"I believe so. Look, could you please leave us alone a moment?"

"I'll get you guys some drinks. Stoli and Coke, Cathy? And you, Jane?"

"Oh, a pint of bitter, please."

Madonna skipped off into the sunny murk.

"Cathy, we could go out, see things, I mean, have fun." Jane's imagination failed her: *Das Kind hat wirklich kein Eigenkonzept vom Spiel.*

Cathy shrugged.

"I'm very sorry, Cathy. I've had every chance in my life, and I'll do everything to make it up to you. Everything I have is yours."

"Bit late, isn't it?"

"No, it isn't. Cathy, it's never too late. I feel, Cathy, I feel as if I've been given a second chance. A second chance that'll make good everything that was bad or wrong. Oh Cathy, do you know what that means? It's miraculous. We're going to have such a good . . ." Jane paused. "Forgive me. We've got lots of time. How old did you say?"

Cathy banged her knees together and said: "You've got to take your opportunities."

Jane sighed.

"Yes," said Jane. "Of course. You're quite right. What do you want, Cathy?"

"I want to be like you."

Jane smiled. "But without the bad things that made me me?"

Cathy said nothing.

Jane stood up. "You can't, Cathy. Life's not like that. I'll give you some money if you want. That's the best part of me." She turned, made for the street door, and tripped over a bar-stool. That checked her. She turned and said: "I'll try again, Cathy, when you're less busy."

At the door, Madonna caught up with her. She was carrying no beer, no vodka, but was replacing a phone card into her Gucci wallet. She said: "Jane, I'd really like to work with you on this. Cathy's sweet and all that, but we . . ." Her face expressed a brilliant future, composed of these things: laughs, money, sensual delight, blokes, taxis, heads turning in restaurants, cocaine, T-shirts from Joseph, beaches in Thailand, tears, violence, unbelievable sexual shame and lethal boredom.

"May I say something to you, Madonna? Off the record."

Madonna took a step forward. There was something new and soft, almost spastic in her movement.

"And I mean off the record. Not unattributable. Not friends of. Off the record."

Madonna looked humidly into Jane's eyes.

Jane said, very quietly: "I'm a killer. Better run." She turned, stumbled again, and passed out into the sunny, dirty street.

During this exchange, Cathy, alone at her brass-dimpled table, had been thinking. She thought: Maybe that old Commie bloke would make a story. I bet he would. I bet I'm not the only one. Ask Madonna. When she comes back. For Cathy, though she had lived a more fortunate life than her brand-new sister, had some of her wit.

On the InterCity back to London, I regret to say Jane drank four miniatures of Haig, which set the exhausted businessmen to coy and literal fantasies, though these were not to be fulfilled: Jane stepped off the train at King's Cross as sad as she'd got on at Glasgow Queen Street. For in the course of that journey, much prolonged by a loss of power at Darlington and engineering work at York, Jane returned in her mind to her earliest years.

And now, much against my will, and overdue, I must tell you about Jane's sadness.

We now enter the inferno of Jane's childhood. I have delayed this step until now, out of my respect for her as a character in literature. Every element in Jane's life served to cover her years of childhood, and if I'd unwrapped these protections earlier, she would be like those men you see in cities, striding along with a briefcase, overcoat and hat – except that it's Sunday in mid-August – and then you see the flapping shoes and ruined shirt and stubble, and know they're roofless, weary, mad.

For the condition of prostitutes in the Greater Glasgow area in the 1950s, Fraser and Bannerman (1958) provides a good, all-round survey. But any study of Jane's particular childhood must begin with the report of the psychiatric social worker, Mary McPhee, to the diagnostic conference of the Glasgow Centre for Child Psychotherapy, usually known as the Heriot Clinic, on 8 January, 1961. This, the first sight of Jane to the outside world, is worth giving in full:

Janet was lying on her side in the corner made by two walls and the floor of the flat, in her vest and pants, masturbating listlessly. She appeared to be between four and six years old. She was cold, extremely thirsty and evidently underfed, and she was bruised on her buttocks, cheek and neck. The flat, which is just one room, contains a bed on which [Deleted] was lying, uncovered. [Deleted] was on the floor by the door, also naked, but a blanket had been carefully tucked in under her breast and legs. The autopsy (enclosure) estimated time of death at not less than seventy-two hours prior to admission.

It was obvious that the child should immediately be taken into care, and that was effected seventy minutes later by officials of the Child Welfare Department and the Procurator's office, Mrs McPhee, and two police officers. The child was admitted to Pollockmains General Hospital and placed on an intravenous course of Vitamin A and Salvanoladine, an opioid analogue then much prescribed.

The question that engaged the diagnostic conference at the Heriot Clinic on the 13th was: What next? Reading the minutes, where at least two of those present suggested institutionalisation, it is astonishing that Mrs Heriot actually advocated treatment at the centre and that Mrs McPhee, with great reluctance, agreed to act as flanking social worker. For how could they hope to succeed with a child so injured, enuretic, encopretic, with very low speech skills, drug-addicted, unable to read, and so listless she would respond to no other stimulus or frustration?

Sisi Heriot *née* Lustgarten was born in Linz in 1908, the only daughter of a family of glove manufacturers that had converted to Lutheranism. After studying at the University of Vienna under Dr Freud, on his pressing insistence she left Vienna on 15 April, 1938, travelled by way of Salonika and Istanbul and arrived in Hampstead in June, where she was put up by the Freuds. Sisi Lustgarten was therefore the last straggler of that group of Viennese intellectuals of Jewish origin that Hitler handed to England like a poisoned chalice, and England accepted with its habitual fairness and indifference. Never was chalice so sweet in the tasting, and so therapeutic in effect!

Sisi worked at first in the War Baby clinic that the Freuds had established at Watlington Gardens, but in 1944 she moved to Glasgow. Perhaps she recognised that with Miss Freud at Hampstead and Mrs Klein at Swiss Cottage, the city was now commanded from its northern heights for the purposes of the psychotherapy of children and adolescents; and also she had met and married, while at Hampstead, the doctor Angus Heriot who was anxious to return to his native city.

Sisi began with a version of the baby and toddler nursery she had worked on in Hampstead, but on the strength of her fortune – her father died in 1946 – and a rather uncertain relationship with the Beveridge Organisation, she began taking on patients including some with parents capable of paying fees. By 1961, when Janet was brought in and, for want of any other solution, housed in the nursery under the supervision of Moira Haddon, the centre had some twenty patients, the nursery, a dozen or so students and some modest research, mostly concentrated on Sisi's theory of Overlap.

Sisi Lustgarten has been criticised – and psychotherapists can be harsh, for they have a very wounding weapon at their disposal – for her theoretical weakness, her willingness to overstep the rigorous boundaries between therapist and patient set by Dr Freud himself, and her childlessness. But in the case of Janet – what was she to do? The child couldn't be introduced to play, and could barely be made to speak. Aged probably about five, she had the developmental age of less than two.

There was no question of transference, for what was there to transfer? The child had grown up as if on a wet moor in a storm of unsatisfied wants, unset limits, gross sexual overstimulation and a parental void.

Mrs Heriot knew, as everybody knows, that you have to be loved before you can love. It is hard to imagine her colleagues comforting a sick child at the breast, cleaning up her piss and shit, or rocking her for hours and hours, murmuring over and over again a verse from Goethe's *Mignon*, which means in English, What have they done to you, poor child?; not from any failing of maternity on their part, but because they didn't believe such things to be the therapist's task; and were anyway extremely perilous. Or teaching a child to speak with picture cards or, later, how to work an abacus. But I believe this early treatment, which cannot truly be described as therapy but was merely *Mutterliebe*, saved Janet's life. And perhaps, if we look deeply into Mrs Heriot's well-organised soul, perhaps it was maternity, rather than any attempt to carry the Freudian method into new territory, that caused her to undertake the treatment.

Naturally enough, this onset of affection and care had spectacular effects. Janet's tantrums burst out of the building and down the street towards Brechin Road; the secretaries clapped their hands to their ears; and for days on end Janet had to be taken back down to the nursery where she came under the distant attention of Mrs Haddon and her listlessness returned. All this was recorded scrupulously, but with mounting excitement, in Mrs Heriot's weekly reports.

There is a pregnant moment when, in working with the cards, Janet keeps selecting those that display the signs Plus (+) and Minus (-). She begins to accumulate and subtract Bayko bricks; and is able to play Snap (though obviously not competitively: Janet's cards are face-up). Eighteen months into the treatment, Janet has an idea of prime numbers. Though not expert in these matters, I feel this was Mrs Heriot's great innovation: that, given the extreme infantility of her patient, it was not a matter of penetrating into her childhood and distinguishing and authorising emotions, but offering a way forward into an autonomous and unencumbered reality: for so, if I have followed her notes correctly, she understood mathematics. By now,

Mrs Heriot had become aware not simply of Janet's intelligence but of a certain power of concentration. A whole week they talked about brown bottles: composed them, subtracted them, either singly (very dark) or in pieces (broken), added to them. Three weeks later, Sisi abandoned the book she was using – a collection of mathematical games Angus had received as a school prize – when Janet wrote up on her blackboard not only the Fibonacci numbers – the shriek of the chalk was murder to Mrs Heriot – but a proof.

Janet was now very frustrated with her speech and the treatment again entered a nightmare of rage and balled-up fists: once she punched Mrs Heriot so hard in the breast that she fell off her chair – an event that Mrs Heriot knew, as she calmly stood up from the carpet and smoothed down her tweed skirt, would be extremely rich in development in the ensuing weeks. She traced the regression to a quadratic equation

$$x^2 - 7x + 12 = 0$$

one of five routine algebraic problems sent each week by the University. Eventually, Angus looked up with the firelight on his face and said, You see, it has two solutions,* my dear.

Sisi didn't answer. Her husband was well used to that. She rarely carried a conversation to a conclusion and often launched into a topic as if they had been discussing it for an hour. If he said something to the point, she nodded vaguely as if the thought had long ago occurred to her, been subjected to examination, and rejected. I'm sure Sisi knew the risks she was running. She knew that, in presenting the child with an image of emotional perfection, she risked delivering her up to permanent disappointment in her relations.

"Time enough," she said, wrongly as it happens, "to sort that out." And then: "You know she tried to reach the house-door, though she was dying. She tried to open it for the child. She tried."

"Yes, dear."

* $x=3$ and $x=4$

By now, Janet was speaking quite well, though in a thick Austrian accent, could recite the entire rural bus timetable of Scotland and go to the lavatory on her own. She still did not, at the age of about nine and a half, know how to read. But her presence in the nursery was now unacceptably analogous and she must be found a home, if only with Mrs Haddon at Motherwell.

Conference felt that she should first learn to read. Mrs Heriot overruled it.

Janet was taken in by Moira and her husband, Denis Haddon, who was shift foreman at the No. 2 spinning line at the QE Works (later assistant works manager). It is to Mrs Heriot's credit that this move, which every sane person would have wished to delay, she proposed neither too late nor at the appropriate time, but if anything too early. Moira Haddon was prepared for the worst and got both less and more: in the room that Denis had fixed up at weekends, which included an IBM calculating machine, Janet stopped speaking again and wet her bed, sometimes a minute after Moira had changed it.

The problem here – and I believe this is not unusual among foster parents – is that the Haddons' marriage was disintegrating. That room with its Santa Claus wallpaper, the winceyette nightgown folded on the cot, the view of chimney-tops and the works, was its swansong. That they were selected as foster parents is, I think, to be put down not to Mrs Heriot but Mrs McPhee, the social worker; though in my heart I know that there was only one place Sisi Lustgarten wanted Janet, and that was with her and Angus in Albert Street: preferably, for ever.

For myself, I would have halted the treatment there, content with its spectacular achievements. Janet was now at primary school, could read (not very well), and could be interested in mathematical problems. But in the course of these sessions, Mrs Heriot must have seen some aspects of Janet's nature that could profit from further work, and though the treatment had tired her – her hair was now completely white – she was not used up, not by a long chalk; though management at the centre, always haphazard, was now non-existent. For Sisi Lustgarten, it was not enough that Janet could now ride on a bus on her own without overwhelming anxiety; that she might one day, probably would, work in a paying job requiring some precision with numbers and no contact with other people, such as sorting at the GPO or, as Denis Haddon suggested, as a book-keeper or quality inspector at the works; that she would, in short, in a phrase beloved of the centre ever since Mrs Heriot had heard it in kirk, "achieve her three score years and ten". But Sisi wanted Janet to be a woman, to love a man or some men, to have a child or children, to exploit her tremendous intelligence and – and here we approach the goal of all these years of work – to be happy.

All through Janet's twelfth and thirteenth years, she saw Mrs Heriot every morning between eight and ten to nine. Some days, she would fly round the room, counting every object in it, multiplying them into numbers that took her half a minute to spit out in front of the chair where Mrs Heriot was taking notes; pulling immense series of primes from the contents of Mrs Heriot's hand-bag; or creating, by an arrangement of furniture that was an agony to watch – *Das Kind hat doch keine Triebkraft* – orders of geometry. I think Mrs Heriot felt now that she and Jane would just sail on and on, till they fell off the edge of the world.

In July of 1969, she received a letter from Hutchesons' Grammar School in Kingarth Street, saying that the school would be happy to give Janet a place for that September, but there was no question of waiving fees, which were twenty five pounds a year and five pounds for uniform. (In Scotland, education is not a gift, for it is valuable.) Mrs Heriot took out the big Clydesdale Bank cheque book and, for some reason, paid five years in advance. At that point, she took her summer holiday with Angus at Loch Lomond and wrote up her weeklies.

The article, *Jane: Some Notes on the Treatment of a Latency Girl*, caused a sensation in the small world of child psychotherapy when it appeared in the centre's *Journal* later that year. It was reprinted in the *Bulletin of the New York Freudian Society*, and later in the equivalent journals in France, Italy, Canada, Mexico, Argentina, Chile and New Zealand. Miss Freud herself wrote to Mrs Heriot, electing to employ German not so much for its clinical precision as for its tenderness. Mrs Klein wrote: "In your authoritative refusal, dear Sisi, to permit the transfer of misery across the generations, I was sent hurrying back to the last play of the *Oresteia*." The Science Report in *The Times*, though short and in some places garbled, was brought to the attention of the Prince of Wales and Mrs Heriot was at last made DBE.

The paper had another effect, which would have brought a frown to Dr Freud's brow. While wholly committed to anonymity in published work, Sisi Heriot had become slapdash, and felt the drop of the final *t* was quite enough to shield her young and vulnerable patient for all time. Also, a sort of coldness had come on her, and she felt she must get something written down. As the fame of the treatment resounded about therapeutic Glasgow, Janet gained an idea that she it was who was being talked about; and, on arriving at Hutchesons' Grammar that September asked that she be written down as Jane Heriot. (Hutchesons' rightly insisted on Haddon, but saw no harm in Jane.)

Though exhausted, Mrs Heriot had no intention of leaving it at that. Though the intensive treatment was over, she was naturally anxious that Jane should safely weather the storms of adolescence, when the emotions are brought to the boil quite as fiercely as in early childhood. Not that Jane showed any sign of growing up – she did not menstruate until she was about sixteen – and the notion that she might attract a man's attention seemed far-fetched: she was a very plain child, fat, with poor skin made worse by sweet-eating, and extremely shy.

In truth, Mrs Heriot harboured a plan for Jane, that never floated into her conscious mind but was nevertheless intensely nurtured, and was wholly inappropriate in a woman analysed by Dr Freud himself: for the founder of the school knew he had uncovered a powerful technology, as later Oppenheimer in New Mexico when he blew up his plutonium, and it must be set about with limits. This plan was that Jane, after reaching university and safely marrying and bearing children, might yet be won in all her strong intelligence for the profession, which had failed to take root in the cold, irrational English soil and, as the Austrians retired or went calmly to their deaths, faced extinction. But long before that, Jane would mature, become touched by sex and interested in the man and woman who had brought her into the world, which last could make or break her personality. (Mrs Heriot was not to know that Elizabeth Bellarmine, in taking

Jane so comprehensively to heart at the time of her sexual wakening, and also offering her the opportunity, in witnessing her death, to mourn her actual and therapeutic mothers, had attempted to perform this service. Such sympathy in a woman who had barely been educated in the modern sense, let alone been psychoanalysed, is near miraculous. It is a sadness to me that, within the covers of a more or less plausible fiction of conventional length, I could not arrange for Jane's two benefactresses to meet; for I'm sure they would have fought like cats.)

On 8 February, 1970, Mrs Heriot was hit by a florist's van in Princes Street and instantly killed. The coroner's inquest accepted the evidence of the driver that she had simply stepped off the pavement in front of him, for there were many witnesses. Jane's adolescence went unsupervised. The clinic immediately fell into a management void. No successor could be found and even the magnificent anonymous gift in 1975 of two million pounds could not stem the slide: indeed, it drew avaricious academic eyes from all over Scotland. (The clinic is now a branch of the Department of Psychology of Glasgow University, with no patients.)

Fortunately, Jane developed very late, and though this made her extremely unpopular with the other girls at Hutchesons', it had two good effects: first, she was not exposed to any emotional storms in late latency and, second, her teachers were obliged to take an expert interest in her. The inspired decision that she should concentrate exclusively on mathematics was taken by Chris McIntyre, the headmaster of the boys' school, in the light of her social ineptitude and the bullying of the other girls but, truly, to torment Ariadne Fisher, his colleague at Kingarth Street, with whom he had a lethal rivalry. But by thus confining her to the operations of pure intellect, they coddled her. Her Oxford scholarship astonished even Hutchesons', a school which since the seventeenth-century had been used to finding lads and lasses o'pairts and sending them south for finishing; though I suspect Mrs Heriot would merely have said, in her thick Vienna accent: "A most appropriate conclusion to your treatment, Janet."

The onset of her beauty – how the fat fell from her, her bust grew, her skin cleared, her hair became silky, her hips rounded – that which astonished and troubled Miss Fisher, as both teacher and woman, so that she said to herself, You'll never be any damn good at this game – and came at such a speed that it had not reached her fingertips, let alone her self-consciousness, at the moment when Johnny first saw her in an Oxford garden, and without thinking, started walking across the lawn – well, it would have interested but not surprised Mrs Heriot. For the woman God made was simply knocking at the door; or rather, as Mrs Heriot would have put it herself, to have accepted femininity in its social aspect gave a mould for the female to develop. Sisi Lustgarten was a great clinical psychotherapist of children and adolescents, perhaps the very greatest, and the Jane case was her best work.

And so, as you always knew, and in the manner of all true romance, my beggar-maid was a princess. For just as Johnny, and the Motherwell seamstresses and Sean McVie and R.W. Turpe, were the last flowers of long social traditions, so too was Jane: in the beauty and severity of her personality, created over years and years by this great doctor of sick children, she was a movement of Mahler, a thought of Wittgenstein, a sentence of Hayek or Popper or Gombrich, a theorem of Ludwig Boltzmann: the last gleaming of that Enlightenment that came down this century upon the Viennese.

You will note that, in this section, I have not attempted to enter Jane's consciousness. That is for obvious reasons. Jane's sufferings in this period are indescribable.

"You scared the wits out of me!"

Beside the front door to the Bagatelle, Jane unbent slowly from her crouch, still trembling, as Johnny Bellarmine took her arm and lifted her up.

"I'm sorry, Jane. I was a little worried about you."

"But how long have you been here, you imbecile?"

He was wearing a white raincoat. He said: "Oh, three, four days, could have been a month. Breakfast at Dino's, lunch at White's, dinner at Milton's. What could be nicer? And I had some work with me."
He breasted a fat folder of tedious paper.

Jane bent and picked up her bag. She said: "Do you want to come upstairs? As they say."

"Have you had dinner?"

Jane was suddenly crushed by hunger, as if she hadn't eaten or at least tasted anything for years. She could only shake her head.

"I've got a table at Milton's." He looked at his watch. "Help! It's time."

"Oh no, Johnny, we can't do that. It's not fair on . . ." She stopped herself. Johnny looked at her stonily. She said: "I'll cook something for us in the flat."

"Do shut up, Jane. We'll leave your things with the porter." He bent down to pick up her bag, and, as he did so, said very quietly: "That doesn't matter now."

"Oh Johnny, I'm so sorry."

He straightened and smiled. "I don't seem to be very good at keeping my wives."

I would like to say that at that moment, as they crossed Arlington Street towards St James's, that Jane, from her privileged knowledge of Johnny's impossibility as a husband, felt some sympathy for Candida, at that time in the air *en route* for Houston, Texas. But the words that formed on her lips looked suspiciously to me like *Silly Cow!* and this interpretation is supported by what appeared next: *Play your cards right, boy, and you might be lucky this evening.*

What she said was this: "I have a sister."

"And I'm your second cousin once removed."

"You are just so incredibly stupid. Don't you understand? It's not that she is but that . . ."

"She wants to be. I know, Jane."

"I've resigned from Textiles and the group, Johnny."

"Resigned! Resigned!" Johnny stopped dead in the St James's traffic. "YOU MUST NOT RESIGN, JANE! Let that old felon sack you." He looked down at her, a little shy. "You'll use Battersby, won't you, Jane?" Battersby was John Battersby, whom we have met before: senior partner at the Lincoln's Inn law firm of Purlingbrook, and said to be at the very pinnacle of his profession. Behind a pose of sumptuous imbecility, he hid a mind both sharp and corrupt.

"No I bloody won't. I don't want any money or a settlement. I want to quit, of my own free will and in my own time."

"And what shall you do, Plain Jane?"

"Oh Johnny, I want to be modern. I'm fed up with the old years. I want to rent videos, and appear on *Question Time*, and have views on women's rights, and go on holiday, and ski, and admire Tierra del Fuego cabernet, and give up smoking, and be on the cover of *Hello!* holding babies, and go to parties and bring blokes home from them."

Johnny nodded, though whether at the catalogue of Jane's modernity, or just some items of it, I do not know. Jane slipped her arm through his. "Business is pretty unforgiving, you know, Johnny. I don't expect I'll run a public company again, and can't say I care. I own a flour mill in Iowa and, now I come to think of it, half an airline."

Johnny stood back to let her pass first into the restaurant.

Once seated in their alcove, which was private without being suggestive, shyness engulfed them. Jane smoked. Johnny attended to the head waiter.

" . . .and a bottle of the Montrachet for the lady."

"Johnny! Half! For heaven's sake."

"I'm afraid, madame, the wine is not bottled in halves. You see . . ."

"Better make the best of it, Jane, while I still have it."

Jane turned to the waiter. "Would you please leave us for a moment?"

"I'll see to the wine, madame."

Jane waited a moment. "I would like to take over your liabilities, if you will allow me. Actually, it's not that complicated. You isolate the old years, ring-fence and fund them, and then walk away. When the American lawyers see the pot is finite, they'll settle. I'll talk to Stephen. And I'll look over his shoulder, Johnny, I promise. Actually, now I come to think of it, it's a no-brainer."

"No, Jane."

"The Wexley thing is even simpler. It costs seventy thousand pounds a year to run, OK, let's say ninety thousand pounds now. Make that an endowment of two million pounds, to be on the safe side, and

Greenwich or the Trust will jump at it. Arlington Street is probably worth seven hundred and fifty thousand pounds on its own: what cause have I to live in a seven hundred and fifty thousand pound apartment! Meg's things. The farm. And Johnny, the public won't want to see everything. They'll have to have the Drawing Room, Library, Chart Room, Dining Room, Huahine, the garden and somewhere to have tea and park their cars, but we could . . . I mean there's plenty . . ."

"No."

Jane hadn't really believed in it.

"You never stop talking, Jane. When we were married, you drove me mad with your chatter. Wexley Park will be sold. My father always said I shouldn't keep it if it became a bore. He strongly disapproved of families living in comfortable country houses at public expense."

"But what about the staff, Mrs Moran . . .?"

This was the housekeeper at Wexley Park, who had particularly tormented Jane during her brief incumbency at that house.

"Pensioners rank above unsecured creditors in a liquidation, as you very well know. What have you been doing these past six years?"

"But . . . But Johnny's books and charts . . . Meg's . . ."

"Jane, you really must stop it. We have to talk about something else. Just this. There are things in the library that Greenwich and Auckland have already or don't want, and the big collectors aren't bothered with, that'll sell at auction for perhaps just ten or fifteen pounds each, so a student could buy something, to have in his or her room. Do you understand that, Jane? A book that Johnny touched and read, that was carried twenty-four times back and forth across the Equator, in there among the paperbacks and CDs. And Meg's property, maybe five quid in a compound lot with coathangers, perhaps even within Miss Stinge's purse . . ."

"Now you stop it."

"Also," and here he looked at her, as if he'd never said such a thing to anybody, or even expressed it clearly to himself – as if he trusted her alone to understand, or help him understand, "you must have learned that money, because of its power to command all things, because it is the absolute means, becomes for us the absolute purpose: replaces love or happiness or peace of mind and even what people used to call God.

My wife believes that money is my personality, and without it I do not exist. I want to try and test that . . . Oh Jane, don't be sad."

He reached out to touch her hand.

"History is quite thorough, you know, and when it wants to bring an idea to the grave, it uses many disguises. The last is comedy and for a very good reason. It is so we are happy to change, and go laughing into the future."

"I'm sorry, Johnny, you know best." She fumbled with a table-napkin. "We will talk about something else."

"Heavens, Jane! Did you see that?"

"No, Johnny. I'm looking at you."

"Tom, with a girl, came in and just went straight out . . ."

"The Age of Miracles has come!"

Now if Tom Burke could find some scrap of tact within him, and that was stronger than his desire to impress his diary secretary and win her for his bed, then so can I. So I withdrew, and sat at the only empty table, and read the *Financial Times*. But I sensed, from across the room, their spirits touch without abrading, and their recollections join without overlap as once their attributes of sex and their polarities of temperament and economic circumstance. As far as I could see, Jane had one and a half dozen oysters and a Dover sole fried in clarified butter; and then, because she was evidently still hungry, a steak-and-kidney pudding, two dishes of *Iles Flottantes*, a disc of Roquefort and a Madeira ice. Slowly, the fumes of gluttony and happiness cleared from her brain. As Johnny piled banknotes on a silver dish, she looked sadly at the remaining Burgundy; but the head waiter bustled up, said, "We'll clean and cork it for you, it's no trouble for us."

Out in Jermyn Street, Jane felt her body transform. Her bust and hips seemed to grow to hallucinatory scale. Her lips pouted. Eyelashes raked her cheeks. She tottered on twelve-inch heels like a financier's mistress. Johnny steadied her with his arm, and took the bottle of wine. It seemed to her that the streets and shops had been lighted just for her, as if she were a hoyden from a rich and backward principality. She wished she lived in Ealing or Slough, so they could go on walking like this all the night.

As she turned into Arlington Street, the bulk of the Bagatelle reared above her, not hateful this time, but home. At the door, Johnny handed her the wine and said: "May I have a kiss, Plain Jane?"

Jane giggled. "You can have more, if you want. Any part of me. Whenever you want."

Johnny turned away. He said: "My mother loved you, Jane, because she saw in you a Meg reborn, who would give our family another two hundred years of prosperity in England. For me, for me, I loved your intelligence, because you saw straight into my heart, and took away this damn pride, and made me forget how fragile you . . ."

"I'm strong as boots. I just had to leave, for your sake, Johnny, as well. I thought if we divorced, you could . . ."

"I know, Jane."

"Won't you forgive me?"

"There is nothing to forgive, my darling. It's just I have some things to do."

"Johnny, I'll help you . . ."

He kissed her on the hair, turned, and strode up the street towards Piccadilly and, as he turned into the crowds, shouted over his rain-coated shoulder, Learn to ski, girl! Jane ran up the street, stopped, then turned round, and walked slowly back down to the Bagatelle. She retrieved her bag from the dozing porter. Riding up to her apartment, she thought: I can't even marry Stephen now. What a mess, girl.

As she unlocked her apartment door, she thought, Why ski-ing, as a matter of interest, then a hand like the hand of God picked her up and tossed her twenty yards. The whole world was sliding unstoppably downwind. Through the horizontal snow, the tail of Kilo Bravo was bucking like an unbroken horse. She tried to kneel and was again picked up and thrown. It was as if the wind had a purpose, which was to separate her from her companions, and then kill her. Something swooped at her, bounced, then vanished downwind: a fuel barrel. The HF radio mast bent double and broke, came at her heart like a javelin, then flew over. Her mouth filled with snow: over the roar of the wind, ice tinkled nonsensically on her goggles. The Otter came up on its tail, the hawser bellying out in the wind like some divine fishing cast, then the airframe burst, the wings sheered and seats, cushions and broken propeller blades blackened above her. Jane screamed, but the words were torn over her shoulder and dispersed at once over a thousand square miles, never to be assembled by human being.

At four, the wind dropped to just forty knots. Jane stood up, rinsed her eyes and face, swept up the broken glass and sponged the wine from the carpet. She stood in front of her Gysbrechts, looked at the skull and glass half-filled with wine and the twist of tangerine peel, and experimented with speaking out loud. She started shakily but picked up. She said: "I'll take you south, when the time comes, if that's what you'd like. It's no trouble for me. I'd like to. I'll go to Oslo or that place in the north of Norway, and learn to ski. It'll be good for me. And I'll put Charlotte's business on the straight and narrow, and marry her to some fabulous *hacendado*, for I know you had a kindness for her, you cheat. You showed good judgement, as usual. Also humanity.

"But it'll be quite expensive, I think, my darling. You see I'll have to lay fuel all down the Peninsula, four or five flights, and the flying season's so short, two months I think. Unless I can get the American Navy or the Chileans to drop it for me, and I don't think even I'm that persuasive. And I suppose the fuel increases in cost geometrically, because the further you go, the more you have to burn to get it there. It'll be a hundred thousand dollars for the aviation fuel alone. And then I'd like the pilots who take us to go away safe and happy, because I've heard there's nothing like it in all the world for flyers, most guys can't do it. And bribes at Heathrow and JFK and Bogota and Punta. There won't be change from a quarter-million dollars. But it's no trouble. That's what money's for. And the other thing."

Then Jane began to sing, very quietly, in an accent that was a mixture of eighteenth-century maritime Northumberland, 1960s Glasgow and turn-of-the-century Vienna, the last lines of the famous whalers' song known as *Lord Johnny's Lament*:

No mouth can say, no tongue can tell,
If my Johnny, with his Lady do dwell.

* *

I wrote this story in February and March of 1994, in three weeks, while waiting for a meeting with my publisher. I had seen Worsley's dream in a biography of Shackleton and I wanted to connect its two terms, commercial London and icebergs, not as an Edwardian nightmare but as a modern romance. I had in mind a phrase of Hawthorne, who thought romance, which frees the writer from minute fidelity to the ordinary or probable, might be a path straight into the heart; and so I invented revolutionaries and countesses and mariners and working-people and members agents at Lloyd's. I wanted to divert a few of my countrymen and women, at a time when they felt down on their luck; to remind them of the variety of English and Scots life; to bridge the chasm between commerce and literature in our country; and to reconcile the bickering sexes. As you can see, it was a no-brainer. It could have been done a million million ways. I did it this way, in February and March of 1994.

As the first week passed, and lunch in London became dinner in New York and then a cup of tea at Frankfurt Airport and then lunch in London again, my characters proliferated and I became interested in their fates if not their putrid occupations. Of their million million possible fates, here are some. Candida didn't stay and who's to blame her; but with her experience of managing large houses and the glamour to some people of her title of nobility, she was not long in the marriage market. After the scandal, Sean McVie did not appear on a platform again but busied himself with his edition of Hegel and travelled to Moscow. He lived to see Socialism in One Country and its concrete expression in Berlin fall down and the orthodox CPGB disintegrate, which I suppose is half a loaf. James Doncaster found no heir to conserve his businesses and serves him right, for he was a mean sod. Lizzie Pinto took to having tea at Eton with the young Prince William. Alan Nixon got Germany right and was translated into heaven. R.W. Turpe and Derek Maughan liquidated their partnership in 1990, but not before they'd extracted for themselves a three million pound dividend each, and retired abroad, one to the country by Siena in Italy,

190

the other to Cocoa Beach, Florida. The case is the subject of an investigation by the Department of Trade and Industry and I can say no more at this stage. Tom Burke fell with his heroine and was reconciled with his wife. Stephen was asked by the Bank of England to oversee the wholesale liquidation and run-off of Lloyd's of London; and for the successful conclusion of this miserable labour, nine years work and not a claim unpaid, he was offered and refused a peerage. I think he lived to a great age; and was greeted by strangers in the streets; and served his country brilliantly alike in peace and war; and came heedlessly to death, as once John Law at the Ridotto, rising stiffly from the tables and stepping down into the enveloping night. Charlotte Meredith farms 130,000 acres (oranges and table grapes) just south of Santiago de Chile. Cathy McKay presents *The Late Show*.

Of the fate of Jane, whose example sustained me in these days without company and nights without sleep, I am not sure. I had planned early on that she should marry Stephen and end the book in an interesting condition: not simply as my homage to the last page of *Joseph Andrews*, but because a girl needs a child to get some respect in fiction these days. But marriage and pregnancy barely scratch a woman's narrative interest, let alone a woman such as Jane. So maybe Stephen should reconsider, for there is, I believe, a shortage of baronesses of colour, and none who is banned for life from the United States securities industry and has served eleven months in minimum-security Federal correctional facilities.

I'm not sure it matters, even to me. For during those three weeks a coldness came on me, and I don't know if it will ever leave me. But I believe what I say. You have to go on as if it all meant something, one more granite shore, one more green inlet leading nowhere, swinging the lead for depth, tasting the water for salinity: till one morning, you feel a cold breath on your face, as if from high latitudes, and you smile, and turn about, and steer dead south, towards the iceblink. And maybe that third person I mentioned is not death nor worldly ruin; but stands in the same relation to me as I to Jane; who dreamed me as I dreamed Jane; and as I care about her . . . ah, who gives a damn?

* *

Live well, Jane, your story is told but for this one last thing.

The pilot dozes on the wing, or skims through *Polar Aviator*, or ducks into the cockpit, on the hour, to take the weather from *Teniente O'Leary*. The engineer fires up the engines on the half to keep the cores from freezing. They don't talk much, these guys. But they think the same thoughts. They think: It's the lady's money, do what she likes with it. It's fine. Nice surface. Five below or warmer. No wind. High, high cloud. Beautiful flying weather. She can take her time. And she's a real nice lady. Real polite. Skis a storm, too, with all that weight.

The lady in question is twenty-one nautical miles away, but she might be under the wing, you see her so clear. You understand that in this unencumbered light you see with the eye of God. You see her, in her blue down jacket, kneeling where no man or animal has ever been in all anterior time, except one. Two skis, two poles, stuck upright in a drift. The little GPS. For the latitude and longitude, you see. And the sled and harness and the body wrapped in parachute silk, whiter than the snow. And the prayer-book and the cross that flashes the unintermediated sun.

You see her rise. Slide into her bindings. Hang over her poles. Snap the empty sled and harness to her waist. Then down the windless air, you hear her say goodbye – just for a while, you understand, not for ever – to her darling.

Terminat hora diem 9 March, 1994